THE CHAIR WHERE TERROR SAT

WILDSIDE PRESS

WEIRD-MENACE #3

THE CHAIR WHERE TERROR SAT - Weird Menace Classics # 3
$5 per copy。
edited and published by Robert Weinberg, 10606 S. Centr
Park, Chicago, Il. 60655

ACKNOWLEDGMENTS

THE CHAIR WHERE TERROR SAT by Arthur J. Burks, copyright
© 1936 by Popular Publications for Horror Stories,
June-July 1936. Copyright renewed 1964. Reprinted by
permission of Mrs. Arthur J. Burks.

BRIDES FOR THE DUST DEMON by Paul Ernst, copyright ©
1936 by Popular Publications for Dime Mystery, December
1936. Copyright renewed 1964. Reprinted by permission
of Paul Ernst.

SATAN CALLS HIS CHILDREN by Arthur Leo Zagat, copyright
© 1937 by Popular Publications for Dime Mystery, May
1937. Copyright renewed 1965. Reprinted by permission
of Mrs。 Ruth Zagat.

DEATH UNMASKS AT MIDNIGHT by Nat Schachner, copyright
© 1936 by Popular Publications for Horror Stories,
June-July 1936. Copyright renewed 1964. Reprinted
by permission of Mrs. Nat Schachner。

FIRST EDITION

CONTENTS

CHAMBER
OF
HORRORS

Welcome back to the world of weird-menaces. It is not
the most pleasant of places, but it is a better one than
the everyday world. At times, with all the horrors that
inhabit these pages, when we compare them with the monstrous creatures who haunt the newspaper pages, we have
to wonder if the creatures of weird-menace are not infin-
itely preferable.
The basic elements of the weird-menace story is that the
evil has to be somewhat logical in nature. That is, by
the conclusion of the story, all the seemingly supernatural occurances have been explained logically. While
there are madmen in these stories, they are usually di-
rected by some sane mastermind out to capture the family
fortune. And, there is always justice and retribution
with the evildoers meeting their just reward. Needless
to say, this is not the way it is in real life.
In trying to analyze why people enjoyed these stories,
various social historians seem to emphasis the gruesome
and gory nature of the tales. This might be true for
some small measure. However, we have to wonder if it is
more because of the very nature of the stories - that
no matter how terrible the menace, the villain is always

4

ultimately brought to justice. These stories, for all
their sex-and-sadism elements are still firmly rooted in
the pulp tradition. Good always conquers evil. There
are no anti-heroes in the weird-menace library. The
men involved (as well as the women) are always heroic -
they willingly fight the most bizarre and horrifying
menaces, often believing that they are fighting an inevitable, absolute, all-powerful evil that cannot be
destroyed by their defiance. With all of their self-
doubts, they never cease to struggle. They never give
up hope. And they never fail to win.
Perhaps this explains why the pulps (or all pulp liter-
ature, even the modern day pulp-style material) have
always been attacked and despised by the intellectual
community. They are upbeat, unrealistic, optimistic -
not a very fashionable way to look at the world, espe-
cially to those who consider the world a dreadful place
where suffering is the rule and norm. The pulps provide
a source of entertainment and optomistic feeling - and
nothing more. In a world bedazzled with getting ahead
by stepping over your fellow man, where cynicism and
deceit are part of everyday life, stories like these
have no believability.
As stated before, perhaps that is why these tales still
retain some measure of their popularity. They remind of
us a day when the world was easier to accept- even with
all of the problems of war and depression. Perhaps the
world was no better then that it is now - but in those
days, at least, we tried not to think so. People still
had faith in certain beliefs and principles that have
been forgotten or betrayed now. It was a time of
heroes, when weird-menaces were always fought, not
applauded, or even worse, ignored. For that reason,
it was a better world than the one in which we live
today.

                           Robert Weinberg
                           November 1977

5

BRIDES OF
THE DUST
DEMON

by Paul Ernst

(Author of "Satan's Flower Shop," etc.)

A Feature-Length Novel of Implacable Doom!

The Dust Bowl—that terrible stage whereon scenes of tragedy and death have been played by the helpless victims of Nature gone berserk, becomes, in this grippingly dramatic terror-mystery novel, the locale of the weirdest, most heart-chilling story ever told!

OUTSIDE the three-story office block, the world was covered with a leaden pall. Dust! Clouds of it —oceans of it—deathly winding sheets of it.

The fine stuff made twilight of early afternoon, with now and again faint glimpses of the sun as a reddened and inflamed ball in a gloomy heaven. The dust sifted in windows that were taped at all the cracks. It clogged lungs burning with weeks of abuse. It weighed down the souls of us who lived in the Dust Bowl of the Middlewest like drifting lead.

Doom! Doom for our crops, our businesses! For our hopes and aspirations! And, just recently, doom for our lives and our immortal souls!

Outside the building, hell-twilight at two in the afternoon. And inside, in the

room where we met—stark horror that went far beyond any emotion, the horrible dust storms that had buffeted our town of Cannersville, North Dakota, could rouse.

The mayor of Cannersville was there; a big man named Purlie, with a paunch and a lined elderly face. He sat near the office window, which was covered with a moist sheet already muddy with dust though it had been freshly hung ten minutes ago.

Behind the desk was Grann, the owner of the business block, and the chief business man of Cannersville. He was thin and stooped, with a greyish face and light blue eyes in which fear rode like a ghost.

Then there were Sheriff Sills, a truculent young man with a walrus mustache; Onnery Holcombe, president and owner of Cannersville's small bank; and myself. I was the only one there who hadn't much of a financial interest in the community. I was manager of the Cannersville Tribune, owned by the widow of the man who had founded it, and that was all.

Grann pounded on his desk with a scrawny greyish fist.

"I tell you we've got to get out of here! We might as well face it. You know how many months we've had these dust storms. You know what they've done to the state—to this whole section. The region is done. It's going to become a desert. We might as well get out now, while we still have a few dollars left, as fight to the end and then be driven out without a penny."

Purlie cleared a throat choked with dust.

"The government weather bureau says it's only a dry cycle we're passing through. Another year, or at most two, and we'll have normal weather again."

"Who can be sure of that?" almost screamed Grann. "Anyway, another two years of this would ruin us all as surely as two hundred years!"

Sheriff Sills tugged at his luxuriant mustache, worn to make a round and vacuous face look older.

"If you're thinkin' of the looting trouble we've had," he said, "I can guarantee that it ain't going to last much longer."

I almost smiled at that. The looting trouble was bad enough. Outsiders, and a few desperate farmers of the community who were near starvation, had taken advantage of the dust pall to strip abandoned houses and also, with violence now and then, to loot houses not yet deserted! Murder had been done, and torturing performed to make men tell where their last few possessions were hidden.

But I knew it wasn't the looting these men had in their minds. Nor was it the tragedy of the dust storms. And Holcombe knew it too, for he said suddenly:

"Gentlemen, we're beating about the bush. Let's say what we're thinking."

THE rest of us looked at him. He was the strong man of the community, I could not help thinking, as I looked at his firm jaw and steady grey eyes. Grann was shrewd in money-making; the sheriff was physically an ox; Purlie was a clever politician and strong in the regard of the Cannersville people.

But it was Holcombe who seemed to have the guts when the world was falling to pieces under our feet.

"We're not talking about the looting or the dust storm," Holcombe said quietly. "Not really. We're talking about the hellish fanatic sect calling itself the Avengers, which has sprung up out of this disaster. We're also talking about the superstition dealing with what the ignorant call the Dust Demon."

There was a silence in the office, with its artificial light dimmed by a billion floating particles of what had once been rich farm land. And no man looked at the other—for Holcombe had brought to light the dark terror which hid in the minds of us all.

The Avengers!

The Dust Demon!

These two dread thoughts were indeed what filled the minds of all of us in the office—of every one in the community, as far as that went!

Holcombe turned grimly toward Sheriff Sills.

"You guarantee that the looting will stop soon, sheriff. Damn the looting! What about the Avengers? What have you done to stop them?"

An awkward sound came from the sheriff's lips. But it didn't form into words. He got red, then pale, and tugged at his mustache again.

Holcombe stared at the rest of us.

"A band of half-mad men and women have grown up around this community and ganged into the most sinister mob this country has ever known. I believe a few of them are sincere. They believe that the dust storms are the wrath of heaven descending on a people who have sinned. They believe that the devil himself has been summoned from hell, in the form of this so-called Dust Demon, to ravage the countryside. They worship this Dust Demon. They take it upon themselves to decide who in the community have been the most wicked, and they mete out a horrible punishment on those who are chosen."

His words sank into a sea of fear that enveloped us all in that dim and somber office, with the dim and somber skies darkling outside.

"The sinners these mad folks choose are those whom they think indulged in carnal pleasures. You know who have been the victims. Young girls for the most part, guilty only of being beautiful and desir-able from a man's standpoint. You know how the victims have been treated."

I think we all shuddered. I know I did. Yes, we knew how they had been treated!

"Barlow, here," Holcombe waved at me, "has seen plenty of violence in his capacity as newspaperman before he came to Cannersville. He can testify, if testimony is needed, that the Avengers are fiends—degenerates. They should be shot down like mad dogs before they get more victims. I . . . I am thinking of my own daughter. . . ."

His voice broke a little, and he stopped. Thinking of his daughter? Well, I was thinking, with as much horror as he could possibly feel, of Evelyn Dawson, the girl I was to marry!

"It's the mad sect, the Avengers, that is running people out of the Cannersville section as much as the dust storms," said Holcombe. "And I, for one, refuse to be run out! Now, what are your plans, sheriff?"

SILLS looked highly uncomfortable. And I didn't blame him. No one knew just who the Avengers were. Every one went around with fear in his heart, afraid that his next door neighbor, the man he spoke to at church, the man who fixed his car, might be an Avenger. They seeped through our whole social structure with their hellish rites, and their awful sacrifices to "propitiate the wrath of heaven and stop the dust storms."

Purlie spoke up. "And what are you going to do about this . . . this thing they call the Dust Demon, sheriff?"

Sills replied to that. "There ain't any such thing," he said. But he spoke doggedly, and with his eyes on the muddy sheet over the window rather than meeting Purlie's gaze.

"No such thing?" cried Grann, face greyer than ever. "Many have seen it. A big, half-glimpsed thing, like a man but not like one, striding through the dust clouds as though it was the spirit of the storm itself. And God knows plenty have seen what the thing has done! You know the claim: The Dust Demon marks for hell's vengeance the sinners to be sacrificed at the Avengers' secret masses."

"Nuts," said Sills, harassed beyond discretion. Then he suddenly remembered Grann's importance in the community. "I mean, how could there be any such thing as a real dust demon? We got troubles enough around here without sending a posse after a thing that can't possibly exist."

"That farmer out Spring Road way saw it," retored Grann in a strained voice. "He saw a thing like a crouching man in a black cape, or with black wings, or something. He blazed away at the thing with a shotgun, and it only turned and came at him. When the farmer got through running and came back, he found his oldest girl not only dead but . . ." Grann shivered. "You know how he found her. She was the second of the people murdered around here. A beautiful girl of twenty! Her father's in the asylum now."

I felt the breath freezing in my throat. I had covered that murder, of course, for my own paper and for several big city dailies who retained me as country correspondent. I had seen the body—once lovely; and I had tried to talk to the father. Mad even then, he was. All he could mumble about was the Dust Demon— "like a gorilla, like the Old Nick himself, with his flaming eyes. . . ." He couldn't even talk coherently about that, any more. He sat in a cell with the walls padded and was watched and straitjacketed frequently to keep him from killing himself.

"Nora Henkel, the seamstress, saw it right in Cannersville," Grann continued. "She saw it go into the little house on Oak Street where the pretty little bank clerk lived with her mother. Marking the girl for slaughter! Well, Holcombe, you know what happened to her!"

Holcombe got up and strode up and down the office, his strong face working.

"Yes, I know. I paid the bill for burying her. And the . . . the undertaker explained why his charge for making her presentable for the coffin was so high."

He swung on Sills with his composure cracking for the first time.

"Damn you! What were you elected for? How far are you going to let these degenerate madmen go before you stop them? And what are you going to do about this thing they call the Dust Demon?"

Sills pulled sullenly at his mustache. Outside the wind moaned and howled as it carried its awful load of dust. Grann coughed as his throat clogged for a moment. And then there were wild steps outside in the corridor, and the office door burst open.

We all whirled toward it. A man stood gasping on the threshold. He was middle-aged, about fifty. His work-hardened hands opened and shut like the grasping hands of a man drowning. His face was lead-blue and his eyes were those of a maniac. I recognized him. He was a carpenter in town named Mackson.

"Sheriff Sills!" he panted. "They told me I'd find you here. Oh, my God! The time I've spent finding you!"

He ignored the rest of us. His wild eyes fastened only on the face of Cannersville's chief law officer.

"What's wrong?" said Sills thickly.

But I think he knew. I think we all knew. Mackson had a daughter. . . .

The words that came gasping from the carpenter's pallid lips confirmed the worst suspicions.

"My girl! My Elena! She's dead, Sheriff! She's been murdered!"

"The Avengers—" Holcombe burst out. The man shook his head. "Not the

Avengers! The Demon! The Dust Demon itself killed her! Oh, my God—"

We all crowded to the door around him, following Sills.

"My car is downstairs," Holcombe said. "We'll take that."

His voice was dull, beaten. And he couldn't be blamed for that. For weeks murder had stalked in our community. Such murder as the mind of man can hardly conceive. Now it had struck again —and again the victim had been a young and beautiful woman.

Wordless, we got into the sedan and started down the main street of the town.

CHAPTER TWO

Mad Murder

IN HOLCOMBE'S car we crept down through the flat small town with the flat great prairies all around it. We couldn't do more than creep at about eight miles an hour. The headlights were on but they didn't penetrate the dust. It was like a fog. No, worse than any fog that ever gathered. For fog doesn't fill your nostrils and parch your throat and make a madman of you with its eternal lashing at raw nerves.

Now and then we saw a man or woman struggling along sidewalks drifted as though with dun-colored snow. They were leaning into the wind with mouths and nostrils protected with cloths, dimly seen specters in the storm.

Mackson sat and whimpered in the back seat. Stark terror rode in his eyes. His mouth was twisted—he wasn't bothering with protecting cloths against the dust. There was going to be another candidate for the asylum, I thought, if this man couldn't pull himself together.

But that was not my main thought. My first regard wasn't for this unfortunate citizen—it was for the thing he claimed had robbed him of a child. The Dust Demon!

The hideous storm around us was like the end of a world—or the beginning. There was something antediluvean about it; something so far removed from our civilization as to be incalculable to the average mind.

Like the great storms of a world's beginning! Wasn't it possible that this tremendous, antediluvean force might have called into being some antediluvean thing as unnatural and as incalculable as nature's tragedy itself was? I'd thought a lot about that recently. And I could not laugh at myself for the fantasy. There undoubtedly *was* some grotesque and misshapen being that walked abroad in the storms, to be seen by horrified men and women occasionally. The Dust Demon was its popular name. The Devil himself, sent to punish the district for its Godlessness, some believed.

I had sent reports to the city dailies that an unknown killer and looter haunted the region. But I didn't quite believe that myself. Living in the dim horror of the Dust Bowl I—I didn't know quite what I *did* believe!

As we crawled along in the sedan only Mackson's insane whimper sounded. None of us talked. It was almost impossible to talk even if we had wanted to. And none of us wanted to!

We got to Mackson's house. It was the last on its street, with the prairie extending itself in the distance beyond. At least it would have extended itself to the eye thus, if the dust hadn't made it impossible to see more than a few feet.

We got out of the car, cloths held close to mouths and noses, and walked up on the porch.

"My God!" Grann whispered.

On the front door of the carpenter's house was a great cross, marked in reddish brown. I saw it closer in a moment, and felt ice touch my spine.

The cross was marked in blood, which

had coagulated a little and was gritty with blowing dust. The mark of the Dust Demon. In every case, before one of Cannersville's girls was killed, her house had been marked like this with a bloody cross. Then the Avengers had come.

But this time the thing had varied. The Demon had evidently marked the house, and then had killed the victim itself!

"Inside," babbled Mackson, fumbling to open the door, while his eyes glared at that horrible sign on the panels. "Inside. . . . In the living room. . . ."

He got the door open at last and we followed him into the house. We moved on leaden limbs, reluctant to see that which we knew we would find.

And in the living room we found a sight to shock the residents of hell itself.

Elena Mackson had been pretty; blond, tall, slender, about twenty-two years old. The thing on the living room floor could hardly be recognized as the carpenter's daughter.

Nude, the body lay, with white flesh all blood-dabbled. There was a huge gash down between her full white breasts, and another gash crisscrossing it.

The character of those gashes caught my attention like a blow. They had been made with something abrasive rather than cutting or tearing. If a dull fragment of rock had been scraped over her yielding flesh with tremendous strength pressing its gritty surface down, the result would have been the same.

My gaze travelled from her body to her head. And then I looked quickly away and wondered no longer at the madness peering from Mackson's eyes. Her face didn't exist any more. The countenance that had been pretty and appealing, was now a red blot, as if a stone had been ground into it by a sadistic giant!

WORDLESS, Grann and Purlie and Holcombe and Sills and I stared at the grisly sight. The work of a mad man!

No, of something not man at all—mad or otherwise! That was my thought, and I believe that thought was shared by the others.

The Dust Demon—a gigantic shadow seen in the dim air of the Dust Bowl, like a spirit riding the storm. . . .

And then—this! With murder marks that seemed to have been made by a gritty surface, and with the cross of blood on the door!

"My Elena!" panted Mackson. "My little girl! She never did any one any harm. She did not sin. It wasn't the likes of her that brought the dust storms from heaven."

He looked with great, empty eyes at first one and then another of us, without seeing us. I can see the look in those eyes yet.

"Me!" he screemed suddenly. "It must have been me! My Elena harmed no one—I must be the sinner!"

He wheeled toward the door.

"It was my fault!" he raved. "My sins have brought my girl to her death and have helped to bring the wrath of God on the country! I am unclean—unclean. . . ."

Before we could stop him, he was gone. We ran after him, out the door and down the hall. He was twenty feet ahead of us when we got to the porch.

He faded into the dust, out of sight. We heard his mad screams and followed him by them. But we were too late.

One last shriek we heard from his unseen lips. Then, as we lunged through the billowing dust, we lunged in silence.

"There," choked Holcombe, pointing. We got to him.

Mackson lay with bright blood pouring from his throat, which he had slashed with a knife drawn from his pocket as he ran. He was already dead, a suicide. Sills bent over his. . . .

The dim, clogged air was split by another scream, from back near the house we had left. We jerked around like puppets on wires. A woman's scream, this was.

"Oh, God, now what?" chattered Grann.

Sills led the way. Again we found ourselves running through the dim and sinister world of dust, like creatures trying to run in a nightmare. We saw a thing all in white, flapping in front of the house next to Mackson's. It looked huge, exaggerated by the dust-laden air. Sills jerked out his gun, but I grabbed his arm.

The white thing was a woman crouching before her porch steps. A woman with grey hair and wild eyes—eyes like Mackson's had been when he staggered into Grann's office.

She was no longer screaming; she was moaning now, and mumbling something in insane accents about her child, her son.

I ran up the porch steps, with Sills on my heels. There was a mark on the door—a cross in blood which was gritty with dust. We leaped into the hallway, and almost fell over it—a stark corpse not far from the front door.

This was a man's body. A young man's body, as we could see from the texture of the nude flesh. You couldn't have told from the face, for it had been treated as the girl's had been treated; obliterated as though a rock the size of a millstone had been smashed down and ground around on it.

"Mrs. Kelsey's son, Jack," Sills muttered.

I nodded. I had recognized the wild-eyed woman too, and I remembered her son, Jack Kelsey. The logic of this attack on him was instantly brought home. The Avengers, following the hellish footsteps of the black storm thing which they worshiped, had always picked as victims those whom they termed "sinners."

Jack Kelsey, young, impulsive, reckless, involved in several minor scandals in Cannersville, would have been just what the Avengers termed as sinful. This was the first man killed, but it was easy to see why such fanatics had killed him. . . .

I brought myself up short, here. The Avengers apparently hadn't killed him! He had been rubbed out, as the girl Elena had been, by the Dust Demon itself! At least the similarity of death-marks indicated that.

And I was set back by those marks, too. I'd seen the marks on the victims of the Avengers, and there were none like this. Mutilation impossible to describe was recorded on those other pathetic corpses. But mutilation obviously performed by human, if degenerate, hands. The marks on these bodies seemed not to have been made by anything human at all. . . .

Sills wild exclamation broke into my thoughts.

"Look! Out that window!"

The windows of this house were not sheet-covered. Evidently Mrs. Kelsey had given up the struggle to keep the dust out. I stared through a grimy pane into a world that staggered in its awful shroud. Through the hideous dimness I seemed to see something else for an instant. Something huge and shadowy—something that moved through the dust fog as though it were a part of it.

"That's it!" Sills choked. "The thing, by God!"

I'D NEVER thought too highly of the sheriff. But I had to admire him now. His face was white, but he plunged to the window, raised it, and tumbled out. I ran after him, toward the great dark shape moving like a sinister shadow of some form of life that existed before humanity began.

There was a garage behind the Kelsey house. We saw the dim shadow slip toward this. Choking in the blinding dust, glaring with red-rimmed eyes, we ran after it. Sills had his gun out.

It exploded as he tripped on something unseen in the dimness and fell flat in the drifts. I avoided his fallen body and went on. I saw something sliding around the corner of the building. . . .

The sight froze me as though I had fallen into icy water. It was what would have corresponded to a hand and arm, if the figure we had seen had been human. But what I glimpsed in that soul-shattering second was not hand or arm.

I saw a sort of claw, twice as big as a man's hand, with but one great, hooked talon on it. And the talon seemed to be of some stuff like rock—*or like solidified dust!*

The Dust Demon—incarnation of the awful storms. . . .

I shouted, then, and would have stopped. But my feet slipped in the dust and I lurched on, past the corner of the building.

Something like a falling beam crashed down on my head and I fell. . . .

The first face I looked into was Grann's, when unconsciousness left me. He was bending over me anxiously, as were Sills and Onnery Holcombe and Mayor Purlie.

Holcombe spoke: "What was it? What happened to you?"

I shook my head. I'd seen the Dust Demon? Been attacked by it? I couldn't get the words out. They sounded too fantastic.

Purlie said: "Sills insists the two of you saw the thing. The Demon. You were actually struck down by it. You must have gotten a close look at it. What was it like?"

I struggled for words, and could find none.

"What did you see, man? Here's a chance to clear up some of this mystery, anyway."

"I saw nothing but a big dark form," I lied. Tell them of the one-taloned claw that seemed fashioned of the dust itself? No, I couldn't do that!

I got up dizzily and went to the sedan. All the questions they showered at me, I evaded. The sight of that great claw sliding out of sight around the corner of the building had stopped my tongue.

"It was the. . . It was *it*," muttered Sills. But no one listened. The men looked at each other in the dim air.

"Heaven help us," whispered Purlie.

"Not heaven—the law!" snapped Holcombe. "These horrors must be stopped before the community is deserted!"

"And your bank ruined," sneered Grann. "That's worrying you more than the human element in this!"

It was said out of raw nerves, and Holcombe must have known it. But he took up the gage.

"It will ruin your business, too," he

pointed out, "and the business of all of us. Certainly I'm concerned about that. Why wouldn't I be?"

The two men glared at each other, then turned to me.

"I'll take you to a doctor's office," Holcombe began.

But I shook my head. "I'm all right. I have to go to the office and write this up. . . ."

I left them, watching the sedan melt into the dust fog a few feet away. But I didn't go toward my office when I started walking, with one hand held to my throbbing head. I went toward the home of Evelyn Dawson, the girl I loved.

CHAPTER THREE

The Call

"**H**EAVEN help us!" had been the whispered words of Mayor Purlie. I could fairly hear them repeated from a thousand pairs of lips on all sides of me as I made my way along the streets of Cannersville. Could hear it from the lips of people cowering behind locked doors which they never opened, these days, if it could be avoided.

The dust in the tortured air grew even thicker, though that had seemed impossible a moment ago. The slight red glimpses of the sun no longer showed. And in this stricken region a thousand homes were swamped with horror.

The sons and daughters of the community in danger! The most beautiful of the girls, and the most promising of the young men, if the death of Kelsey were any indication, stricken down without warning! None knew whose door would be next marked by the bloody cross—whose offspring would be next to go. In farm homes on the prairie, in houses in the little town, crazed parents speculated about that in tones of terror, and never let their families out of their sight if they could help it.

There was only one indication, one guide: The victims, marked for the Avengers by the bloody cross or, as in the case of the two whose young bodies I had seen cold in death, killed by the thing itself, were always good looking, popular, clever young people. The kind the Avengers called "sinful."

It was this indication that had driven over eighty farmer parents of good looking youngsters from their farms—a thing not even the dust storms had been able to do. It was this guide that had made forty families flee from the village itself, leaving friends and homes and everything else in their horror of what had happened.

And it was this guide, this indication, that was now driving me half mad with fear for Evelyn.

The girl who was shortly to marry me was by all odds the most beautiful in our community. This was not just lover's prejudice; she had been judged that in a state beauty contest a year and a half before, in which she had almost won the title of Miss North Dakota.

She was what some of the pinched old folk of a backward region speak of as brazen and forward, because she dressed in nice things bought in Chicago, read books that were heresy to fanatics, and wore a one-piece suit when she swam in the town pool. She smoked cigarettes, too; and once a sewing circle gossip had seen her drink a glass of wine with her uncle, Doctor David Dawson, with whom she lived.

Beautiful, progressive, alive—Evelyn was only too hideously the type picked on by the unknown Avengers. Fear had torn at my heart for her for days; and now, hastening from the sight of that great unhuman claw, I found myself running through the murk as I neared her house.

And I could have yelled with relief when her door opened to my knock, and I saw her face.

"Darling!"

"Bill!"

She kissed me, face white and strained as were all faces in this community of fear. Then she exclaimed. "Bill, you've been hurt."

"I tripped and fell," I lied. "Can't see where you're going in this dust. Has . . . Have you been all right here?"

"Of course," she said quickly. Too quickly, I thought. "What could happen to me? You don't think I'm worried about that ridiculous 'Demon' some of the more ignorant farmers believe in, do you?"

But her lips were white as she spoke, and I felt her tremble a little in my arms.

"Evelyn, for God's sake take care of yourself," I blurted out, with the vision of Elena Mackson's hideously marked body in my mind.

"Of course, Bill! But what could happen to me? Uncle Dave is a dead shot, and we're always together."

"He has to go out on a call once in a while," I said miserably. "You're left alone then."

Evelyn shook her head.

"You see? You've been worried over nothing. When he goes out on a call these days—I go too. Right with him! So you needn't be afraid for me any longer."

She took my arm.

"We can't stand here talking when you're hurt. Let me do something about that gash in your head."

SHE took me into the study, and there her Uncle David Dawson growled a greeting. A big man with greying black eyebrows, he wasn't as busy now as he was accustomed to being: folks didn't

even open their doors to a doctor now, unless they were very ill indeed.

Dawson bound up my head. "Hit by a rock, eh?" he commented. And then Evelyn and I went back to the front room. We sat down there, with her hand in mine and both our hands tense.

We didn't say much. We looked at the window, covered by the inevitable moistened sheet. It was almost as black as night out now, though the clock on the mantel said only a quarter of three. Dust an eighth of an inch thick covered everything in the room, though Evelyn cleaned thoroughly every day.

"Evelyn," I said suddenly, "let's leave all this. Let's get out—start over in some more decent place. Why do we stay here and fight the elements—and everything else—when we could live east or west of here and get away from this damned dust?"

She looked at me, and I felt a little ashamed. But I plunged on:

"I could get a job on a Chicago paper, I think. We could be married at once, have an apartment there on the lake—"

I stopped. And she shook her blonde head slowly.

"You don't really mean that, Bill. You wouldn't really—run away. Why this is our home! It was lovely once, and it will be again, when these storms stop. You have a chance to buy a paper of your own here—the one you work on now. And Uncle Dave's practise is here. We don't want to leave a grand scout like him, do we?"

I moistened my lips.

"But besides the dust, there is this maniacal crew that calls itself the Avengers! And there's the thing they call the Dust Demon—"

"The Avengers are human, Bill. I guess we can fight anything human. And as for this creation they worship, this bogey that goes around marking crosses of blood on doors where new victims live—I guess we can forget that. It's only a thing of insane imagination. Probably one of the Avengers makes the blood marks on victims' doors. Besides, no one has ever seen the 'Demon' has he? Well, then?"

"Several people have claimed they saw the thing," I said, avoiding her eyes.

"Pooh! You know yourself how objects are distorted by this fog of dust. You can see a half-buried tractor, and think it's a monster. No, until some one reliable actually sets eyes on the thing, I refuse to be afraid of it."

I swallowed. Would she think me reliable? What would she say if I told her of that horrible claw I had seen—and felt as it crashed down like a rock club on my skull? But I said nothing about that.

"Let's just go away for a few months, then," I urged. "I have enough in the bank to get us married and give us a four or five months' honeymoon—"

The ring of the phone stopped me. I listened in a cold sweat as I heard Doctor Dawson answer. In these dreadful days, a ring at phone or doorbell, a call in the night, a shout in the whirling dust, could mean anything—usually tragedy and horror!

"Yes, this is Doctor Dawson speaking," I heard the doctor say. "William Eno? Yes, Will, I hear you. You want me to come out. . . . You what? *What?* . . . Great God!"

I ran to the hall where the phone was, with Evelyn beside me. Dawson stared at us with eyes fear-fixed.

"The door of the Eno home got the mark of the blood cross. Will Eno says he saw the thing that marked it—just a glance in the dust as he was coming from the barn. He saw something big and dark, bigger than a man, and it seemed to be made out of the dust itself. It slid out of sight as he got near—but he saw it. Then he ran into his living room to phone."

DAWSON wiped great drops of sweat from his face.

"His girl, Margaret! She was in the kitchen, he says. He heard her out there. But when he went back from phoning, she was gone! His wife, the girl's mother, lay unconscious on the floor. She'd been struck by something. Will phoned me to come out and tend to her. He's leaving the house now with his two hired men to try to find Margaret."

Dawson was struggling into a rain coat as he spoke. Lots of us wore raincoats; they helped to keep a little dust from powdering us all over when we went out. He jammed a grimy hat on his head.

"Uncle Dave—I'm going too!"

"Not this time, Evelyn! Not out to a place where this thing—man or fiend—has just struck," Dawson said.

"I'd rather go there with you than stay here alone."

"I'll stay with you," I said to her.

But she shook her head, with her eyes frightened but resolute.

"You've got to cover the story out there, Bill. Besides, I'll be all right—I won't leave Uncle Dave for a minute."

"You have a gun?" I said to the doctor.

He nodded. "And I'll use it at the first excuse! Come on, you can ride out with us."

We hurried to the door. I opened it for them, and we stepped onto the porch. I started to close the door. . . .

With the greatest effort of my life, I kept a cry like that of a scared child from coming to my lips. I covered the door with my body as they started down the steps, so they couldn't see it. And as Dawson started his coupé, I kept talking to Evelyn so she wouldn't happen to glance back.

On the door was a mark. A great cross,

dabbled in blood that had coagulated a little already and was gritty with drifting dust.

CHAPTER FOUR

The Storm Devil

THE bloody cross on the door of Evelyn Dawson! My girl marked for slaughter! That was all I could think of as the doctor's car dipped and rolled like a ship at sea over the dust drifts on the concrete road.

I couldn't have maintained normal conversation to save my life, with that dread thought in my mind. Fortunately I didn't have to. All three of us were gripped by tense silence as Doctor Dawson raced toward the latest scene of disaster. We hung on while the coupé pierced dust clouds through which no eye could see for more than a few feet. The doctor was finding the road by instinct.

We got to the cross roads called Mechanic's Corners. Beyond here a short distance was Eno's farm. We bored through the blinding dust till we came to big concrete gateposts, beside which was a rural mailbox marked William S. Eno. Dawson turned in. . . .

A world sheeted with dust! But through it, now and then, a glimpse could be had of the great barn thirty yards away, and the house about the same distance to the left.

The barn, the house—and something else! Something that seemed to swim, like a great fish almost unseen in depths of water, through the storm. Something the sight of which gripped me with such horror as I've never felt before or since.

A great black shadow like a man in shape, and yet with a sense of something dreadfully unhuman about it!

My hand clenched over the side of the car. Evelyn felt my convulsive start, and must have seen even in the dimness how pale my face was.

"What is it, Bill? What's the matter?"

"Nothing," I said. The dim and awful black shape was no longer to be seen. I wasn't even sure that I had seen it, now. "It's just the dust, and the things that have happened. I'm jumpy, darling."

"Who wouldn't be!"

Her eyes went somberly to the Eno house as the coupé stopped in front of it. And my gaze fastened on her pale, lovely face.

The bloody cross on her door—and out here, haunting the scene of the latest tragedy, was the thing the Avengers worshiped—the thing that had filled the whole community with horror such as few communities have ever been fated to know!

I was going to get Evelyn out of this region, at once! As soon as we got back to town from this trip! On that I was resolved. Meanwhile. . . .

No one greeted us on the porch or at the door. I remembered Dawson's statement; Eno had said he was going out to scour the countryside for Margaret with his hired man. We went in at once.

"The kitchen, he said," Dawson ground out.

We went down the gritty hall carpet to the kitchen and opened the door. Then Dawson leaped forward.

On the floor beside the sink lay a middle-aged woman, Mrs. Eno. There was blood on the floor and on her head. The blood on her head had been washed away with crude gentleness, but some more had oozed forth—from a great gash on her left temple. A clumsy bandage was on her head, and a pillow was under her. Eno had tried to help her before going out to look for his daughter.

"She may live," Dawson said, examining the ghastly wound. The woman's breathing sounded horrible, stertorous, in the dust-filled atmosphere. "We'll give her first aid here, and then rush her in the coupé to the Cannersville Hospital. Water, Eve."

Evelyn stepped to the sink. She was white to the lips, but she began to help her uncle as composedly as a veteran nurse.

"Clean cloths."

Evelyn drew a basin of water, and got an old sheet which she began to rip up. I went to the kitchen door.

"I'm going out and look around," I said, keeping my voice as steady as I could.

Dawson only nodded. "Don't be away long. We'll want to rush Mrs. Eno in as soon as we're through here."

I went out of the kitchen and down the hall to the living room. There was something in there, over the fireplace, that I'd seen on our way down the hall, that I wanted. That thing was a shotgun, evi-

dently an extra that Eno hadn't needed when he went with his men to look for his daughter.

I got the gun down and broke it. Both barrels were loaded. I went to the front door and out into the dust-filled world.

Unless my eyes had been playing me tricks—in a light and atmosphere where eyes *could* play tricks on you—I had seen the Dust Demon haunting this spot. I wanted to see it again. Now! I wanted to see if it was unearthly enough to be able to stand a double load of slugs at close range!

I STOOD at the foot of the porch steps with the gun held ready in my hands, and looked around with dust-smarting eyes. You couldn't see the gateposts from here. But off to my left, as I faced the road, was the great vague shape of the barn. I went toward that.

THE CANYON OF MISSING BRIDES by ARTHUR J. BURKS

Ahead of me I suddenly saw a shapeless form squatting low in the murk. I brought up the gun, covered it for a moment but held my fingers on the triggers. I took slow steps forward.

Then I grunted and straightened up. The thing in the dust was inanimate: a wagon buried to the hubs in dust.

Sound shrilled through the air. It came from the barn, and it raised the hair on the back of my neck. It was the screaming neigh of a frightened horse. But there was an eerie quality in it as though the fear behind the animal cry were not a normal fear.

Again the frightened neighing sounded, with the same weird tone in it that you hear in the howl of a dog when some one is dead nearby. I started toward the barn. . . .

The first thing I saw when I got within ten yards of the barn was a smear of blood and flesh and feathers on the ground. I stopped. It was a chicken, looking as if a steam roller had passed over it. No, looking as though a rock had been ground wantonly down on it—as the face of Elena Mackson had looked.

I bit my lips and went on.

The barn door was open. And that was odd. I knew that Eno wouldn't have gone off with all his men leaving the barn door open like that. Chill touched my hands as they clenched on the shotgun.

In the barn, the neighing horse suddenly seemed to go mad I heard the thunder of flying hooves in a confining stall—then silence. Ghastly silence, with no more neighing and no more hoof beats.

I went into the barn as a man moves to his execution. For I was certain, now, that the mysterious thing which rode the dust storm was within. But—I kept on going. If that black beast, whatever it might be, could be killed, the community would be rid of the worst half of its horror.

I walked past a row of stanchions in which cows, gaunt from drought-parched feed, were moving uneasily. I went past a box stall, and saw a horse standing, trembling in every muscle. The next stall. . . .

I stopped with an exclamation ripping from my throat.

There was a horse in here, too. But this one was not standing. It lay in the straw, dead, with its skull crushed in. It looked as though it had been hit just above the eyes with a sledge hammer.

Or with that terrific, stony looking claw I had seen back at Mackson's place!

From the rear of the barn came a sudden sound. It was like a step, ponderous, slow, in the hay. I walked slowly toward it through the mist, with the gun taut in my hands. Hinges creaked, and a moment later I saw that the great rear door of the barn was open, too. I went out. . . .

Instinct warned me, I guess, for I heard no sound. I whirled to the right, and there I saw a great black blur of movement. Shouting hoarsely I leaped back as a claw swept toward me.

For an instant I could make no further move, as for the first time I saw the thing at close range, with all its hideousness stunning my gaze. I couldn't even bring the gun up.

I saw a figure a foot taller than any man, with the bulk of a gorilla, and with one-taloned claws, like stone hooks, instead of hands. It was covered by black flapping stuff of some sort like loose hide. But its face was its worst horror.

I saw a face like a nightmare mask carved by a drunken sculptor out of dust-colored rock. There was no forehead, a misshapen blotch for a nose, a mouth like a slit cut in stone. Great dull eyes stared out of this incredible face, and the stony looking talons raised toward me.

These things I saw, made more terrible

by the slightly concealing dust veil between us. Then I jerked up the shotgun and pulled both triggers. . . .

THE slugs went up in the air as I was pulled violently backwards. I saw the black storm horror seem to melt into invisibility as it faded backward into the shrouding mist, and then I stared at things almost as hideous—things that had crept up behind me as my senses were dazed by the sight of the Demon.

They were figures of men, shrouded in some sort of grey stuff like sacking. The men were masked; and on the masks were crudely painted skulls. Through the eyeholes in the painted skulls, their mad eyes could be seen.

The Avengers! That dread disguise of theirs had been seen all too often around Cannersville. They had been near the spot where the black thing they worshiped was lurking. And—they had got me.

I clubbed with the gun, but felt the stock seized and wrenched away from me. One of the men came close. His insane eyes glared into mine, and the painted skull on his mask moved as the lips beneath uttered words.

"Kill him! He tried to harm the storm spirit!"

Many hands grasped me, now. I struggled against them, but was held as if I'd been a child. The strength of the mad! I'd heard of that; now I experienced it. Lunatics all, these masked men were. But at least the fear they inspired lacked the final dread touch of the supernatural which was inspired by the thing I had seen a moment before—like a giant gargoyle carved out of caked dust.

"Kill him! Kill!"

Their hands were tearing murderously at me. One raised a club and brought it down. I ducked just enough to keep from

being brained, and felt my right shoulder go numb as the club smashed down on it.

Then, abruptly, I felt some of the pressure of the gripping hands ease up. And at the same time I felt the eerie horror that had been mine before.

A great black shape loomed indistinct in the dust clouds. The dust monster had come back.

"Our Master," shouted one of the masked figures. "Down!"

On hands and knees, the group abased themselves before the half-glimpsed monstrosity with a face such as a child might carve crudely in dried mud. I was yanked down with the rest. But now only two men held me, one on each side.

"A sign, Master! Shall we kill this man? Give us a sign!"

I saw the great thing sway a little in the wind like an uneasy animal . Could it understand the words flung at it? I couldn't guess. And I didn't take time out to try. For the grip of the man holding my left arm was distinctly less forceful than it had been a minute ago.

"Avenging spirit that we worship—a sign—"

I wrenched with both arms, moving the right in a haze of pain, and leaped to my feet. Yelling, the two who had held me, lunged for me, but I got back as their scrabbling fingers scraped my legs. And then I was gone, racing back around the barn with the Avengers after me.

I rounded the corner, leaped dust drifts that would have recorded my footprints, tried to tread only on earth scoured clean by the sobbing wind. And then I ran— not toward the house—but back into the barn again.

I raced up to the hayloft. From there I could see the house, just barely, and could see that Dawson's coupé was gone. He and Evelyn had started back to town with Mrs. Eno, so they were safe from these maniacs if they searched the house for me. I went to the other side and looked out. There was no sign of the black thing. Again it had faded into the storm, after the sight of it had chanced to save me from the Avengers.

I crouched up there, and, after a long time, I saw the crudely disguised figures come back around the barn and start off through the storm to some unknown destination. Then I crept down, and following their tracks in the blowing dust drifts, I pursued them.

No man knew where these fiends met for their hideous worship. If I could find out, and lead the sheriff back with a posse, at least some of the bloody tragedies of the region might cease.

CHAPTER FIVE

Satan's Cathedral

HOW can I describe the stealthy pursuit through the murk of the maniacs calling themselves the Avengers? I'm afraid I can't. No one who has not been in the heart of the Dust Bowl when a strong wind blows could get the picture. Fine silt drifting on the ground as fine snow drifts; piling up around scrawny weeds, half-burying buildings, filling the air so that the eyes are blood-shot and aching and the lungs scream silent rebellion! And up ahead of me, figures now and then remotely seen which were as much a horror of the storm as the blowing dust itself!

I didn't follow closely; I dared not be caught now when there was a chance of tracking them down. I followed mainly by their prints in the dust; prints which would not last five minutes in the screaming wind.

We crossed a farm that I knew to have been abandoned two weeks ago. The tracks I followed led around a tractor, buried to the radiator cap, with ploughs somewhere behind it. Then they led up to, and over, a fence that sent a thrill of incredible discovery through me.

It was a high fence of mesh instead of barbed wire; the kind of fence you see on estates of rich men. Only one man in the country had fence like that around his great farm. That was Mayor Purlie.

And as I climbed across the fence to take up the track again, I knew, suddenly, where it was going to lead me.

On the far corner of Purlie's two-thousand acre farm there was a huge, abandoned barn. The house accompanying the barn had burned down long since; the farm it had serviced was one of six that Purlie had bought and thrown together to make up his own acreage The big building had never been torn down; it stood, bleak and unused, far from the road, unvisited by any one.

I was willing to bet that the Avengers used this barn as their dread chapel; and the bet was won in another few minutes. The tracks I followed led across dust drifts to Purlie's barn! And as I got near, I saw other tracks, made in the dust recently by other groups going into the place.

This was the spot, apparently, and it looked as though even now a meeting of the Avengers was gathering. I started to turn away and hurry to Cannersville for Sills and deputies. But I was not yet sure, and I had to be before I reported. This was too vital a chance to break up the sect to risk making mistakes.

I heard voices through the reeling murk, and threw myself down in the dust. Two figures passed within ten yards of me; two of the masked Avengers. One went directly into the barn. The other paused in the doorway for a moment, then appeared with a broom and began to obliterate the footprints in the threshold dust where the wind would not perform the task for them. I crept closer, his back turned, and I leaped.

One hoarse exclamation came from his lips and then I had my hands around his throat. Bestial snarls came from the mouth under the mask. Fingernails raked at me like the talons of a mad beast. But his struggles weakened, and then subsided. I kept my grip for a long time. . . .

The face under the mask was stark when I drew the mask off. The face of Jed Somers, an auto mechanic in Cannersville. Bloody foam was on his lips; even in death his face had a brutish, hideous, inhuman cast.

I dragged the body to one side and took the grey, sacklike stuff he wore over his suit. This I slipped on myself, and then I put the mask in place and went into the barn.

It was impossible to put the atmosphere of that place into words, though I feel it vividly and clearly even now.

A big empty barn always has a strangely churchly air. The roof is so far above; there is such space, such quietness. This had the same air, but it was an air perverted! This was like a cathedral, but a cathedral of hell, with the atmosphere seeming charged with pure evil.

A T one end I saw a bulky thing under a shrouding black cloth. Before this were forty or fifty masked figures, kneeling and gesticulating wildly. Mad cries came to my ears, and slobbering as of worshipers gone insane. Then a sort of hymn burst forth—drum beating music of the devil. And finally, all got up.

I walked toward the group, praying that no detail of the coarse cloth that shrouded me would be different from the others. For if I were caught in here I knew there would be but one answer.

A figure leaped up from the others suddenly and stood before the black-draped object. An object, I notice, that was taller than a tall man and twice as bulky. The figure began to rant; and at the sound of the voice I recognized him.

He was Ezekiel Snaith, a former preacher of the district unfrocked for blasphemous practices.

"Brethren and sisters," he roared, with the painted skull on his mask fluttering to the words, "you are met again to mete punishment on those whose wickedness brought the disaster of the dust to our fair community. Once more we follow the will of the storm devil, our master, in annihilating a person who has leagued herself with the devil, and damned men to perdition with her pretty face and body. Do you agree that we sacrifice this person to placate Heaven and stop the dust?"

Voices which were hardly human screeched and bellowed an answer. The answer was in the affirmative. All heads moved forward, and I started to turn and steal away, for I had learned plenty now. But then a sound stopped me. It was a small sound, after the Avengers' ravings, and I would not have heard it except for the fact that a taut silence now held the unholy crowd.

The sound was a girl's sob. And I craned my neck with the rest—to see a girl being half carried and half dragged from behind the shrouded black thing by two big men.

She seemed either hurt, or dazed with fear, for her limbs hardly moved as they brought her forward. Her face was chalk white. Her long hair was in loose strands around a body that gleamed soft white in places where her faded gingham dress was ripped.

I knew the girl. Margaret Eno; the daughter Will Eno sought even now.

Two men dragged her in front of the black object, facing the crowd. Glazed, dull with horror, her eyes played over the masked, cloaked crew.

"Here is a Jezebel whose doings shame

the district," roared the masked ex-reverend. "Small wonder that Heaven's wrath descended upon us when such as she is allowed to roam free and destroy men's souls. What is your will concerning her?"

The crowd roared at once. I felt the men on each side of me tremble with mad rage and lust and unholy ecstasy. Beyond the man on my right I heard a woman's voice coming from behind a painted skull.

"Kill!"

"Destroy!"

"Throw her to us—we'll fix her!"

"Humiliate her first!" That last was in the woman's shrill tone. And the swaggering figure that led the gathering heeded it more than the others.

"We shall shame the Jezebel who till now has known no shame. Then we shall destroy."

I stood there, burning with rage, not knowing what to do. The horror of holding this girl—simply because she was young and lovely! For Margaret Eno was innocent enough. She danced at the Cannersville pavilion now and then. She had dates with young men as any girl does. That was all.

But to this mad crew she was desecration itself. Their insane rage and their anxiety to placate the storm gods would know no limits. And I was powerless to help! One against forty or fifty, I would be killed in a few seconds if I tried to intervene. That would mean that no one could lead men against this infamous place where degenerates "worshiped."

The two men who held the girl tightened their grip. I saw their fingers sink into her bare and shapely arms, saw the white flesh turn raw and red where it bulged. The leader of the sect stepped to her. His hand hooked under the neck of her dress and he pulled.

The girl hung there in the men's hands, with the front of her dress gone. Her white breasts gleamed in the murk. Her body glowed palely to the waist, where sheer silk still veiled her a little.

The sheer silk went the way of the dress. The girl hung there nude, like a drooping lily. And still she did not scream or struggle. It was as if she were utterly paralyzed by the incredible terror surrounding her.

"This wanton," roared the big man leading the sect, "this woman of loose morals! This traitress with the seductive body!"

His hands passed over Margaret Eno's nakedness, slowly, with mad relish And the Avengers surged forward a little.

"It is your wish that she be sacrificed to appease the heavens?"

"Yes!" was the roar.

"Then unveil the god so that he may see the sacrifice."

A figure leaped to the black, shrouded object directly behind where the girl stood in her odd lethargy. A hand went out to the shroud. It was a woman's hand, I saw, even in the dimness. The rumor that many women were in the horrible cult of the Avengers, was only too true.

The hand jerked back, revealing what the shroud had hidden. . . .

Great God! It was the Dust Demon! The hideous thing I had seen twice this afternoon!

TALL and motionless it towered there, like a graven image, with its crude and almost featureless face staring out over the heads of the mob. Like a weird gorilla covered with loose and flapping hide, swinging single-taloned claws instead of hands at its sides.

There was a moan of fear and awe, and the crowd went to hands and knees as the Avengers had out by Eno's barn. The great thing made no move of any kind to acknowledge the abasement. It simply hulked there, an object of nightmare horror in the murk, with the girl's slender white body drooping like a broken flower before it.

And now I saw the sect's infamous leader draw a knife from under his rough cloak. And that was more than I could stand. It was to the community's good that I leave this girl to her fate and get back to give word of the meeting place. But—I couldn't do that.

I was near the wall of the barn. There were loose boards along this wall, blown in by wind during the years of its uselessness. I caught up a narrow, hewn plank about four feet long.

Still, all around me, the dread Avengers were on hands and knees in abasement before the curiously docile Dust Demon. They did not see. No one saw the movements of one of their masked and cloaked number with a crude club in his hands— till I got within a few yards of where the girl was held.

Then there was a roar from the men holding her, and the rest straightened up with shouts and curses coming from their masked lips.

I sprang forward. The bellowing leader rushed with knife upraised, but my club caught his arm. I heard a snap like that of a breaking stick, and saw him fall, with a broken arm. Then I was clubbing the two who held the girl. The others were rushing forward. I got the two, and whirled with sweeping club to keep the others off.

All the time I kept expecting fatalistically to feel that monstrous thing they worshiped bearing down on me, blasting me into oblivion with one of its terrible talons. I got to the girl's side.

"Run," I yelled. "I'll try to hold—"

I stopped. Slowly the girl was sagging, with eyes closed. And as she fell, I saw why she had not struggled in the grasp of the men. In the whiteness of her back was a great stab wound. She had been

mercifully almost dead when she was dragged in front of the monster. And she was beyond all helping now.

The Avengers were all around me, now, save in the direction of the black thing. I leaped that way, swinging my club with all my strength. I smashed the club squarely across the head of the Dust Demon. . . .

The head disintegrated as though it had exploded. And it disintegrated, not into any sort of flesh and bone fragments —but into clouds of what seemed to be *dust and dry earth!*

Then I was leaping over the incredible substance of the thing and had gained a small door behind it. Panting for breath, almost unable to realize that I was leaving that place alive, I ran through the blinding dust with the Avengers streaming after me.

But in the dust, all the cloaked figures looked alike. I went around the barn and mixed with the figures still streaming from the door and after me. The nearest pursuers plunged into the press, striving to distinguish the hunted figure from all the other figures that were identical, save in height.

Near me was a man of about my build, as far as I could tell under the concealing cloak, I pointed at him.

"There he is!" I shouted. "There's the one who desecrated our master's meeting place!"

With mad shouts, they clubbed him down. They swarmed over his prone body like flies. I didn't know who he might be —but I did know that nobody would ever be able to identify the mass that had been head and body when they got through with it. . . .

After a moment, when it was safe, I turned and stole off in the swirling dust, shivering with revulsion and nerve reaction.

CHAPTER SIX

Capture

THROUGH the murk which blanketed the world like an endless nightmare, I blundered on the way back to Eno's farm. It was on the way to town anyhow, and I remembered seeing a light truck in his barn which I intended to take for a dash to the village. If Eno and his men were back, I would tell them of the Avengers' meeting place so that they could guard it till I returned with Sills and a posse.

But Eno was still out, somewhere in the wild hell twilight, when I got to his place. House and barn were standing vague and empty, like sinister dream buildings in a brown snowstorm. I started the truck and backed it out.

I missed the gate in the blinding dust, and ploughed through the front fence. But it was light, of palings, and went down without hurting the truck. I got onto the highway and started toward Cannersville.

Ahead of me, every minute or so, I could see a faint trace of other tires. Another few minutes and even these would be washed out by dust. But now they still showed a little: the tracks made by Dawson's coupé. Doctor Dawson and Evelyn would be home by now, unless they had stayed at the hospital where they were taking Mrs. Eno. . . .

I swerved the truck suddenly as a sprawled object, already dust-shrouded, showed at the side of the road. I started to go on, though I knew what that object was, then got out of the truck cab.

The object was a corpse, all right, even as instinct had insisted. The body of a woman. And I bent over it with a pity that swiftly turned to a numbing horror.

For the corpse was that of Mrs. Eno, the woman Dawson and Evelyn were to have taken with them to the hospital!

For a full minute, absolutely stunned, I stared down at the body which had been tossed like a discarded paper sack onto the side of the road. Then I got back into the truck and began tearing toward town at a pace that threatened momentary disaster.

I was shivering like a man in a chill, then. I couldn't feel the steering wheel with my icy hands. Mrs. Eno—tossed from Doctor Dawson's car! I knew why. My heart screamed in answer. Though my brain refused as yet to accept that answer.

And then I saw another pitiful dust-mound by the side of the road, and skidded the truck's tires in a desperate stop.

Another body! Another corpse! But this was a man's. And at sight of the face, with open eyes and mouth already filling with the all-pervasive dust, I groaned out curses that were like prayers.

It was Doctor Dawson, Evelyn's uncle. His face was intact. But the back of his head had been pulped as though by a grinding millstone—or by one of the tremendous claws of the thing I had smashed back at the Avengers' meeting!

The second body tossed from a speeding car! And here the faint tracks of the coupé turned from the road. I followed them for a hundred yards across a field, then lost them for good.

But their direction in that short distance sent me tearing over the dust-filled prairie hummocks back toward Purlie's abandoned barn!

Then had her! The Avengers had Evelyn! I bucked over the rough fields till the truck shrieked and moaned with the strain of the jouncing. I sent its wheels clear of the ground, on sharp dips, in my awful haste.

Evelyn—in the grip of the masked men before the rest, victim of mad superstition and storm-exaggerated lust! I could hear the cry of the woman in the barn;

"Humiliate her first!" I could see some one taking the place of the man whose arm I had broken, ripping her garments from her before she was "sacrificed. . . ."

I drove too fast. The truck's front wheels hit a fence post too solid to break. The truck careened, and overturned. I was thrown out. . . .

I staggered to my feet, dazed for a moment but not hurt. I went on toward the barn, feeling the dust sting against my cheeks. The skull-painted mask had been torn off me; that was all. Though I don't think I would have felt any hurt short of a broken bone, such was my frenzy to get to the barn where Evelyn was being held. If she were really there. . . .

BUT I was sure she was. I had covered my tracks, awhile ago, by drawing suspicion on the man the rest had clubbed to death. I had done it to keep them from deserting the barn and finding a new hidden meeting place, as they would have done had they known a trespasser had lived to get away. That same covering move would make them think it safe to take their latest victim, like the others, to their regular rendezvous.

I got to Purlie's mesh fence, climbed it, blundered along in the dust. I got near enough to the barn to see it like a great wraith of a building in the murk. And then I saw something else. A thing I knew was impossible—and yet which I knew was there!

God in heaven! The thing! But I had killed it in the barn. I had shattered the bizarre substance of which it was made, had seen its head fly to clodlike bits. Was it able to reassemble itself again? Was the stuff of which it was made immortal?

I tottered there in the dust clouds. And the thing came toward me. Then I turned to run but my legs refused to bear me up.

The next instant a thing like a rock club dashed down on my skull.

The dark dust-world went pitch black, then faded completely out. . . .

A droning of voices penetrated slowly to my returning consciousness. Then another sound—a voice I knew, crying my name.

"Bill. Bill!"

I opened my eyes.

"Bill. . . . Thank God you are alive!"

I was lying on a rough wooden floor. Lying within a yard of me was Evelyn.

I SAW her eyes, wide and fearful in dimness. I saw her lovely body bound by harsh hemp rope which had rubbed livid marks in the whiteness of her wrists. I tried to get to my feet and succeeded only in making bonds around my own body bite deep into my flesh. Two figures, trussed like fowl for market, we lay there.

The insane gibberish that sounded like and yet unlike people chanting in a church, rose monotonously to my ears—the worship of the Avengers. We were in their crude chapel.

"Evelyn, darling! How did you. . . ?"

Evelyn shuddered.

"Uncle Dave and I started away from the Eno place soon after you had left to look around the grounds. I was afraid for you. I wanted to wait. But we had to get Mrs. Eno to the hospital. We were driving along about a half mile from the house when Uncle Dave saw a man's body lying in the road. He couldn't go around it—wouldn't have anyway. He stopped to see if the man was dead, or only injured. Two other men, in the garments of Avengers, jumped from behind a dust drift and got him. . . ."

Her voice choked up, then went on.

"They dragged him back in the car, and held me. They put him in the rumble seat with sacking over him, and a little later they threw his body in the ditch. I think he was still alive. But then I saw—a great black thing rise out of the dust and go to where he lay—" She hesitated.

"I . . . I don't know what the thing was, Bill. I don't even want to guess. The coupé went on, and I didn't see it, or Uncle Dave, any more."

She stared at me. "Did you take that road before they got you? Did you . . . see Uncle Dave?"

I wanted to lie to her. God knows I did. But I have never been able to lie to Evelyn.

"My God! He's dead," she whispered, after a long look at my face.

She closed her eyes. Tears seeped from between the closed lids. I thought of the irony of events.

While I had been in the "chapel" of the Avengers, more of the hellish sect had been out trapping the girl whose door had received the sinister blood mark. They must have brought her in here shortly after I had stolen away. A matter of only three or four minutes, probably.

As for the appearance of "the great black thing" near Dawson's car—I gave that up. It was almost certainly the Dust Demon Evelyn had seen. But how could it be out there—and back here in the barn at the same time? Was it able to dematerialize and materialize at will?

"Where are we, Bill? Do you know?" Evelyn said, with her eyes still closed.

"We're in an old barn on a far corner of Mayor Purlie's farm. The Avengers meet here."

Evelyn got a little whiter. Her lips trembled. But that was all. She took it like a little soldier. I was flooded with admiration and love for her—and with horror at what these fanatics soon would do to her. Futilely I struggled with the rope that bound me. . . .

Out in the main part of the barn, the gibberish of mad chanting stopped. There was a sort of concerted, eager snarl, and then the sound of approaching steps.

Figures tramped into our line of vision. Figures of the Avengers, with their bodies cloaked and their faces hidden by the skull-faced masks.

"This is the Godless pair. Take them. Bring them to the altar."

The seeping stickiness at my wrists became copious flows as I tore skin and flesh on the rope there. But still it held. Rough hands jerked Evelyn and me to our feet. We were dragged into the barn, and toward the waiting crew by the end wall.

CHAPTER SEVEN

Hell's Rites

HIDEOUS figures surrounded us, with a rustling of the coarse fabric that made their cloaks. Mad eyes peered at us through eyeholes of painted masks.

Then we were thrown to the floor in front of the spot where I had smashed my club into the huge black form these degenerate fanatics worshiped. There was nothing there, now; the Dust Demon was not in attendance.

Evelyn's voice sounded, freighted with terror, but almost calm.

"I guess this finishes it, Bill. I . . . love you."

"I love you, Evelyn."

Two of the Avengers stooped and jerked Evelyn to her feet. I bit my lips as I strained at the ropes. The two men dragged her before the masked crowd.

A man of medium height stepped up to the two men who supported Evelyn. She hung in their arms as Margaret Eno had hung, almost motionless. There is such a thing as an anesthesia of horror. I think it drugged Evelyn and I was glad.

The man taking the place of Snaith, whose arm I had broken, faced the snarling, degenerate fanatics.

"You are looking at one of the most conscienceless sinners in our community," he shrilled. I thought for an instant I recognized the voice. It sounded a little like the high tone of Grann. But that, I knew, was impossible.

"This wanton has committed all the cardinal sins. Chiefly that of exhibition. She attended the godless contest in which young ladies, dressed only in one-piece bathing suits which exhibited their bodies shamelessly, were judged for the brazen beauty. It is small wonder that catastrophe has fallen upon us—and our course is clear: remove this source of contamination as we have removed others. . .

"This hussy glories in exhibiting herself," sneered the man taking Snaith's place. "We shall humor her before we send her soul to hell as a hostage. Then we shall be ready for the blasphemous scribbler who is her consort."

His hands shot out. His fingers clutched the front of Evelyn's dress as Snaith's fingers had clenched in Margaret Eno's. He ripped downward.

I heard a pitiful small moan come from Evelyn's lips, and then I heard things in a daze, and saw through a red mist. I yanked at my bonds as though my flesh were of steel and could feel no pain at all.

Dimly I heard more ripping of fabric, and through the red haze I saw Evelyn's nakedness like a white and lovely flame in the murk. The glittering eyes of the Avengers were like pawing hands as they leaned forward toward that ivory beauty.

Now there was a whip in the head Avenger's hands. I hadn't seen him pick it up. All I saw was that it was there. It curled like a slim snake as he cracked.

"Wanton!" he screamed. "Your lewd flesh yearns for caresses. It shall have the caress of the lash. Your body yearns for white-hot ecstasy. You won't look the same when your black soul finally leaves its carnal dwelling place and goes down to the flames!"

He brought his arm back with an expert snap of the wrist, and cracked it forward. The whiplash sang through the air. There was a hissing thud, drowned out in a scream torn from Evelyn's pallid lips.

I shouted hoarsely myself, with the cry lost in the roaring of the blood-lusting Avengers. A thin red line crossed Evelyn's white body just under her breasts.

"There's a caress for you! *And here is another—*"

The dread lash snapped back again. . . .

I WAS on my feet, swaying like a mad animal with streaming almost fleshless hands flexed before me. The roar of the crowd changed to a furious bellow, and the man with the whip turned. The lash sang through the air toward my head.

The rope that had bound me lay in coils around my feet. It had been looped around my ankles in a continuous hitch and tied at my wrists so that every move I made to free my hands twisted the coils around my legs tighter. But the pressure released at the wrists, the whole binding had fallen away.

I caught up the coils of rope as I stooped to let the lash hiss over my head. I leaped toward the man with the blood-flecked whip, swinging the rope in mad hands.

I swung it at the leader's masked head. The snapping coils got him with a sound that cracked out even over the mob's roar. He screamed hideously, and sagged to his knees. I snatched the whip.

God that was good—the feel of that whip! In a detached corner of my mind there was the foreknowledge of doom, of sure death in a few moments. But in the meantime I had that heavy whip in my hands, and before me were drooling things I would cut to bits. . . .

Lashing with the whip, I met the rush of them. The snarls changed to screams as the lash left great red smears on skull-painted masks.

Then there was a circle around me. From somewhere outside of it I heard Evelyn's shriek.

"Get away!" I yelled to her. "For God's sake—"

I had no more chance for words. The ring around me was closing in, in spite of the awful lash. A powerful hand caught the lash at last, held it even though it was cut deeply through the palm.

I reversed the whip and brought the weighted butt down on the man's head. There was a crunch, and he dropped. But other hands had caught the trailing lash, now, and I was disarmed. The Avengers swarmed over me.

Then I was down on my knees. Hands sought for holds in a dozen places. Fingers pressed like iron around my windpipe. I heard it only as a distant roar, like blasting heard many miles away. I fell forward stupidly on hands and knees as for some reason the screaming mob turned from me.

And then I knew the reason, for I could hear better when the next roar sounded—the savage blast of a shotgun fired from near at hand.

Through pain-hazed eyes I saw four men at the other end of the barn. They had shotguns, which were pointed at the crew. One of the men was Will Eno; and the others were his hired hands.

As I stared, the gun in Eno's hand jumped deliberately. I saw his white, wild face blotted out by spreading flame from his gun muzzle for an instant, then saw it again as he started to fire once more.

"Hold it, Will," one of the other men said. "We've winged aplenty already."

"But they killed my girl!"

"I know. But leave the rest for Sills."

I couldn't get up. Flooded with the power of three men a moment ago, I was as weak as a kitten now.

I saw half a dozen cloaked forms writhing feebly, like wounded snakes, on the planking; saw three more that did not move at all. The rest of the crew were milling around like cattle.

There was a touch at my shoulder. I looked up. Evelyn was beside me, utterly unconscious of her nakedness in her frantic fear for me. One of the four men stooped warily and dragged the cloak from a dead Avenger. He tossed it to her and she thanked him mutely with her eyes and put it over her white shoulders.

Then, over the moaning of the dust storm outside, came the sound of many voices; and more men came into the barn. There were over a dozen—Sills, and deputies. They were dragging a thing that wrung a groan of superstitious dread from the lips of the Avengers. A brutish, unhuman thing with a face like that which a child might model out of dried clay, and with dull, staring eyes. The Dust Demon.

"Got 'em, huh, Eno?" grunted Sills. "I'd 've been right with you, but we saw *this* in the dust and stopped to take it."

"Here's the one responsible for the whole damn thing," Sills ground out. "He only got a few of the many killed himself. But he handled these dummies, the Avengers, like a club to kill others. He just marked crosses on their doors, and the mob did the rest, lettin' him walk around as he pleased because they worshiped him."

His hard hand swept out and crashed against the creature's head. It came off, and fell to the barn floor, where it cracked in two. Then Sills gripped the black "hide" at what seemed to be the Demon's headless shoulders, and pulled. A leathery mantle fell away—and revealed the white, frightened face of Onnery Holcombe, Cannersville's banker. . . .

EVELYN lit a cigarette for me. I couldn't work it so well with my hands wrapped in bandages.

"But if all the people around Cannersville left because of the reign of horror," she said, wrinkling her pretty forehead, "it would wreck Holcombe's bank, wouldn't it? I don't understand—"

"Darling," I said, "his bank was wrecked anyway. The drought did for that. He was going to win back personal wealth by driving people away from their farms and taking them over for the proverbial song. He had learned what most people around here still don't know: The government is going to buy this land, at good prices for reclamation."

I puffed at the cigarette, which Evelyn held for me.

"I don't suppose he dreamed he'd get in so deep, at first. Then, as the Avengers got out of hand and did mad things, he went all the way in his campaign of horror to empty the community. When he went to mark the door of Mackson's daughter, he was surprised by young Jack Kelsey and the girl together, and had to kill them himself, instead of just marking them for slaughter. When he went there with us at first, he slipped away in the blinding dust for a few minutes and became the Demon by holding his raincoat up over his head and letting the distortion of the storm do the rest He fooled me with that plaster-of-Paris 'claw'."

"He sledge-hammered Eno's horse and then saved me from the Avengers—that time—so I could get back and write horror publicity that would help his devilish campaign. He marked you for killing because you and your uncle have talked many people out of leaving the district and he wanted to stop that. A cold and ruthless man—a killer when he'd once had a taste of it."

I shut my teeth hard.

"I thought I'd killed the 'Demon' when I smashed that mud statue the Avengers had made of him. I was sure I'd gone mad when I saw the thing again—"

Evelyn stopped my lips with something much more acceptable than a cigarette.

"Darling, let's don't talk of it or think of it any more. Holcombe's on his way to the chair, the deluded fools he organized are behind bars. . . . Kiss me."

I kissed her again, and the dust in the room seemed to change to specks of gold as a dim ray of sunlight entered the taped window. It didn't matter any more, anyhow—the dust. It would stop some time. And my wife and I would help the community build over again. . . .

THE END

SATAN CALLS HIS

It was nothing to Jennie Gant that she chose a path which led straight into horror beyond human imagining, or that she was surrendering her lovely, youthful body to savage lusts that could breed only in evil darkness. For her little brother was in the hands of Satan's henchmen—and she was going to his rescue. . . .

CHAPTER ONE

Where Horror Brews

THE air lay thick and steamy against Jennie Gant's thin cheeks, against the round firmness of her bare arms. It sapped the crispness from the

CHILDREN

By ARTHUR LEO ZAGAT
(Author of "Death Breaks Quarantine," etc.)

A Feature-Length Mystery-Terror
Novel of Ancestral Fear and
Deathless Menace

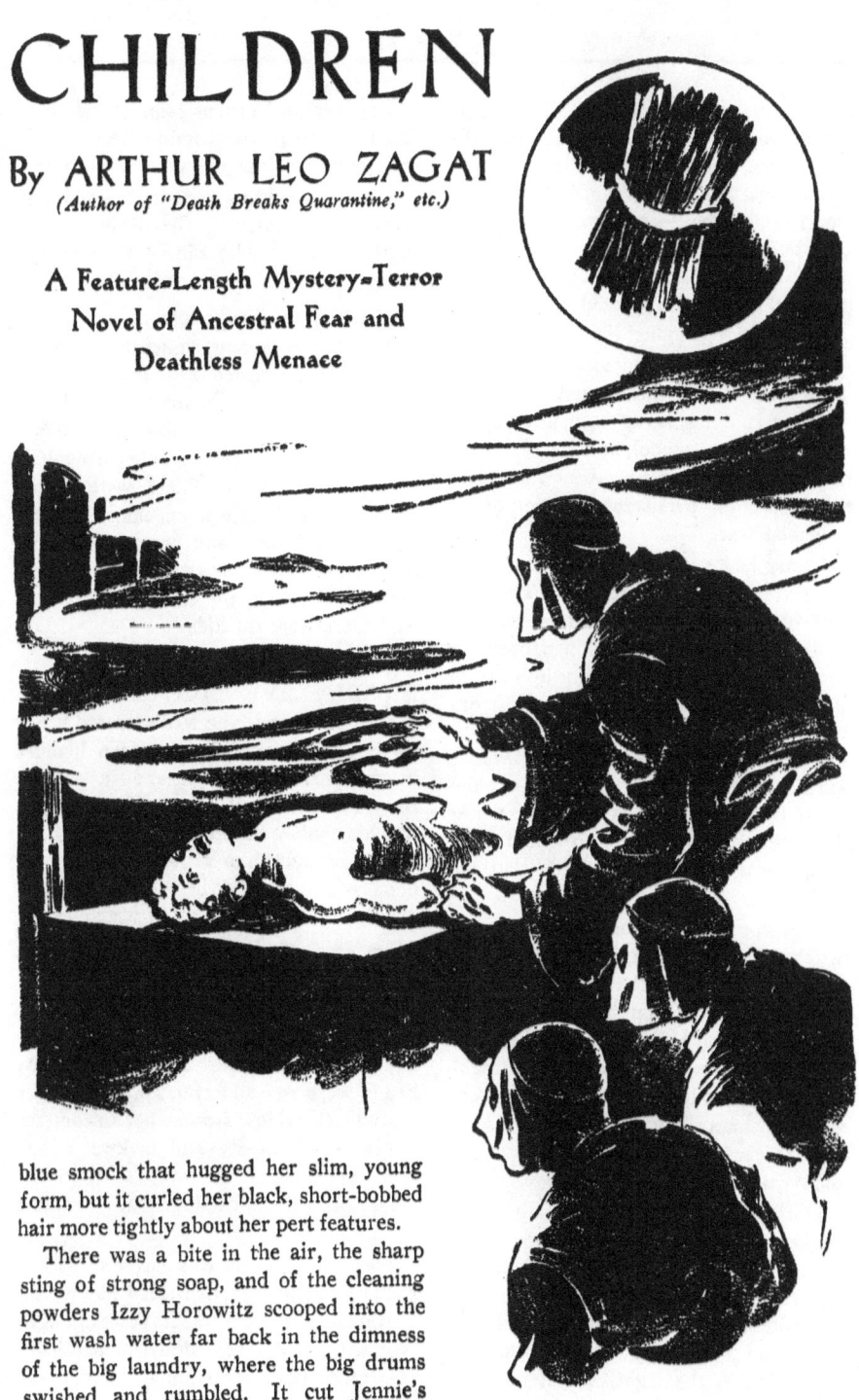

blue smock that hugged her slim, young
form, but it curled her black, short-bobbed
hair more tightly about her pert features.

There was a bite in the air, the sharp
sting of strong soap, and of the cleaning
powders Izzy Horowitz scooped into the
first wash water far back in the dimness
of the big laundry, where the big drums
swished and rumbled. It cut Jennie's

nostrils, and throat, and made her cough.

She would keep on coughing after she went home, and Dickie, her little brother, would look at her with big dark eyes too worried for his seven years, till she kissed the worry out of his eyes, telling him it didn't mean anything, telling him that all the girls who worked in the Super-clean Laundry coughed like that.

Bob Coffey wasn't so sure the constant little hack didn't mean anything. Bob was just studying about occupational diseases in medical school, and last Saturday he had talked anxiously about the weakening effect of "persistent irritation of the bronchial tract."

Jennie had used the soft argument of her velvet lips to silence Bob. Thinking now of Bob and Dickie, while her deft hands stripped damp stockings over the hot metal leg standing straight up in front of her, and stripped them off again dry and gleaming with the soft sheen of fine silk, the sureness of their love was a warm ache in Jennie's breast. She wondered if the Garden Avenue deb whose sleek legs this gossamer web would cover tonight was half as rich in affection and tenderness.

The corners of her wistful mouth twitched bitterly. The deb didn't have to slave from seven in the morning to five-thirty at night so that her small brother might have clothing to warm him and food on which to grow strong and straight. The deb's sweetheart didn't have to spend his night patrolling a warehouse down by the river to keep himself alive till this long years of study should be over.

Jennie's right hand picked up a wet stocking from a basket to the right of the silvery gleaming leg, and slid it onto the leg. Her left hand slid it off and tossed it into another basket at the left while her right hand picked up a wet stocking from the basket to the right, slid it onto the leg. . . .

The Boss had picked Jennie to work at this machine in the window because she was good to look at, and good at her work.

It was nice sitting here to do her work. It was nice watching the different patterns the sun made, sliding through between the ties of the Morris Street "El."

There were always lots of people out there, queer-looking, queerly dressed. There were bearded old Jews in long black coats and round, shiny hats. There were Sicilian laborers, collarless, swarthy, their white teeth flashing under drooping, tar-black mutachios. There were shambling, tired-looking women, shawls hooded over faces brown and wrinkled as the coconuts on the pushcart near the corner, sharp eyes roving the carts for bargains. And there were the kids.

MARIA LEVENITCH came along the sidewalk, pushing a dilapidated baby-carriage. The threadbare brown blanket in the carriage was tucked in around Baby Andros so all you could see of him was his chubby little face, just waking up. Maria brought him around every afternoon when she did her marketing, and would stop here so he could watch Jennie work while he crowed at her and flapped his sweater-covered arms at her.

Maria was stooped over the carriage as if she couldn't straighten from bending over the washtubs all day. Her bony hands were red and cracked. Under her rusty-black widow's dress her uncorseted figure was scrawny and awkward, and she walked as if she were so tired she would drop if the carriage wasn't holding her up.

Her round head was covered with a shawl and she was dish-faced like all the Sylvanian women. But Maria wasn't ugly. Not when she looked down at her baby. Her pale eyes were shining. Her weary mouth was touched with a quiet sort of smile, all love and pride and tenderness. The smile made her almost beautiful.

She stopped the carriage right in front of the window. Little Andros tried to get up, but the blanket wouldn't let him. His mother went around to the side of the carriage and pulled it loose.

The baby's arms darted eagerly out of confinement, reaching to be picked up. Some makeshift toy was clutched in one little hand, and Jennie's throat went dry as she saw stark, utter terror flare in Maria's face.

For a minute the woman didn't move at all but stared at Andros, her eyes like holes somebody's thumb had dug out of her dough-white, quivering mask of a face. Then her suddenly blue lips opened, rounding, and though Jennie could not hear her, she knew the word they shaped.

"No!" Only that. But it was a soundless cry of agonized protest.

It seemed to free Maria from the paralysis that had seized her, for all at once she snatched the toy from the baby's hand, dashed it to the sidewalk with a strange fierceness, and then had Andros in her arms.

She held him to her, so tightly that his little body flattened the pillow of her breasts, so tightly that it seemed she was trying to crush him back into the safety of her body from which so recently he had come. She showered kisses on his face, on his tiny lips that were puckering, uncertain whether to cry or laugh.

Jennie's hands kept moving in the mechanical routine of their work, but she didn't know it. She knew only that she was staring at a mother's unexplainable anguish, at a mother who was—unmistakably—kissing her babe farewell!

Was it the thing Andros had held that had terrorized Maria so? Jennie looked for it, saw an unconscious foot kick it toward the corner curb. It was just a bundle of small black sticks the thickness

of wooden matches and twice as long, tied together by a narrow ribbon of gray fur. The girl's eyes came questioningly back to Maria.

In the instant they had been away from her, a change had come over Maria. She seemed more controlled now, and there was a hardness about her face as if she had come to some decision. She had put the baby back into the carriage and as her work-worn hands covered him with the blanket they lingered with an odd reluctance.

She straightened, and looked around her with peculiar furtiveness. Then she was wheeling the carriage toward the corner, a peculiar slinking stealth about the way she moved. Like that, Jennie thought, a rabbit must appear, sneaking toward the safety of its burrow with a fox in sight that had not yet spied it.

The carriage reached the curb, stopped there as a towering truck hurtled from the direction of the river to cut off Maria's strangely furtive flight. Maria's bent arms straightened. . . .

And deliberately she shoved carriage and baby over the curb, straight in front of the thundering truck!

HORN blare, a shout, hammered against the glass through which Jennie saw this. Wood splintered under huge, skidding tires. A wire carriage wheel bounded crazily across the cobbles, hit an "El" pillar and spun. The truck lurched to a stop—too late.

A woman screamed.

Morris Street pelted toward the corner, toward the rocking truck, toward the jumble of splintered wood under its wheels that was being swiftly died scarlet by an infant's blood. Morris Street shouted, in a dozen foreign languages; screamed, and streamed toward the corner where a baby's life had been blotted out.

Maria was on her knees. Morris Street

thought she had slipped on a banana peel, on some bit of slick debris dropped from a pushcart, and that in falling she had thrown the baby carriage forward to its destruction.

But Jennie Gant knew different! Her fingers all thumbs on the door latch, getting it open and throwing herself out into the screaming, shouting street, she knew she had seen murder done. Jostled and bumped by people running too fast to look where they were going, she knew she had witnessed the planned, deliberate murder of a babe by its mother whose love for him had been a white flame glorifying the ugliness of a pushed-in, flat face.

She reached Maria, still on her knees with nobody looking at her because they were too interested in what was going on in the gutter. Jennie bent to her.

"Why?" The girl's voice was hoarse because her throat was so tight. "Why did you do it when you loved him so much?"

Maria's eyes lifted to her, and they were like the eyes of someone who had died. "No," she husked. "I slip."

"You lie!" Jennie saw the bundle of black sticks on the ground right by Maria's knee. She picked it up and shoved it almost into the woman's face. "You killed because of this, because of something it told you." She knew, all of a sudden, that this was so, just as surely as she knew her own name. "What did it tell you?"

Maria's lips were like gray worms writhing in her gray face. They whispered: "I no have the money to buy heem from Satan, so I geeve heem back to God."

CHAPTER TWO

"Bury Her Sin!"

JENNIE GANT couldn't quite believe she had heard the words. They meant nothing, or they meant something so hor-

rible she didn't dare understand them.

The terror was back in Maria's eyes that looked past Jennie. Her face was livid and her mouth was twisted open as if she were shrieking, but she made no sound at all. Jennie caught the terror, so that spinning around to see what it was that Maria looked at, she threw her arm up to defend herself from. . . .

From what? There was nothing, no one, on the sidewalk to be afraid of. There was only more people; men, women, kids; running to join the crowd at the corner, panting because they had run so far and jabbering questions at each other as they ran. They bumped each other, but they didn't bump one figure that paced calmly along the sidewalk. Even in their excitement they twisted and veered so as not to come too near him.

He was tall and thin, and his black silk cassock emphasized the somehow awesome dignity of his slow walk. A big black cross dangled from a chain of black beads that came out from under his square-cut, long black beard. His features were sharp and hawk-like, his black eyes burning with a brooding dark fire under the black-tasseled, diamond-shaped black hat he wore.

He was Papa Anton, the priest of the Byzantine Church on Hogbund Lane where the Sylvanians worshipped in the mysterious manner of their mysterious, homeland where Europe and Asia come together at the top of the map.

Where the Sylvanians worshipped! Maria was a Sylvanian, and. . . .

Something tugged at Jennie's hand! No, not at her hand—at the fur-tied bundle of sticks she held, plucking them from her startled fingers. She whirled, saw a flurry in the crowd as someone plunged through it, already hidden from her by the jostling, excited backs.

A wordless cry came from her throat.

She dived after the one who had stolen the little fagot that was the key to what Maria had done.

Jennie shoved frantically at those stubborn backs, whimpering, "Let me through. Let me through." She thrust her slim, trembling frame in among them. Shoddy cloth rasped her cheeks, her arms. Unwashed bodies stank in her nostrils. Someone swore at her. She pounded against a back that wouldn't move out of her way because it was squeezed so tightly by other backs on both sides of it, and the crowd behind shoved against her, so that she couldn't move.

Jennie sobbed, knowing that the one she was after had got away. Or maybe he was one of those who was squeezed against her in the crowd. How could she know? He would have the sticks hidden, and it was only by them she could tell him from the others.

Through rows of craning necks she saw the high side of the truck rising and swaying and moving backwards, and she heard a gasp from those in front who could see what the big wheels were being lifted from. . . . All of a sudden there was a loud crack behind her, like a backfire. But it couldn't be that because it came from the sidewalk.

EVERYBODY turned to that sharp sound, Jennie too.

Maria was folding over forwards on the pivot of her knees, and there was a great hole in her forehead over her left eye, black edged and scarlet-centered. Her right hand was falling faster than the rest of her, as if the weight of the gun it held was carrying it down. The belt holster of a motorcycle cop who was bending over Maria was empty. His hands were still reaching out to help her up, and surprise was just coming into his big-boned, weather-bronzed face.

Someone shoved in front of Jennie, so she couldn't see any more, but the whole story of what had happened had been there, in that second of stopped motion that was like a still in the lobby of the Palace. The cop had bent to help Maria get up and she had pulled the gun out of his holster and killed herself.

It wasn't because she had murdered Andros that she had done that. She wouldn't have bothered to make it look like an accident if she had meant then to kill herself too. She would have gone under the truck's wheels with the carriage. She had sent a bullet crashing into her brain to escape some punishment she hadn't known was coming to her, till the

---

moment she had looked past Jennie and terror had flared into her face.

Was it for saying what she had to Jennie that she was to be punished? Jennie was certain now that the sticks were a clue to what had threatened the baby. That was why they had been snatched out of her hand.

Some movement in the crowd, some accident in the way it surged to get to this new excitement, to lap up this new sensation with its thrill-thirsty eyes, shoved Jennie out of it; so that she would have fallen over Papa Anton, kneeling beside Maria's sprawled body, if the cop hadn't caught her arm and held her.

The strong feel of his fingers on her elbow, his blue uniform and his silver badge in front of her eyes, calmed Jennie a little, cleared her head. She must tell him what had really happened, that Maria had killed her baby purposely, and why.

"Get back," he growled. "Get back and give the father a chance." And he shoved her against the shoving people behind her.

"Wait," Jennie said. "Wait. . . . I want to tell you. . . ."

"Let the sin of this poor lost soul be buried with her in her grave," Papa Anton's deep voice boomed out, drowning her gasped exclamation. He was praying for the dead, but why was it in English he prayed? Why did his eyes—almost on a level with her own, he was so tall— catch hold of hers so fiercely and burn into Jennie's brain? "She is now before her Judge, and it is not for you who yourselves will so soon be judged to condemn or absolve her." Then he was touching Maria's breast with the black cross he wore on a black chain, and the booming syllables that came from his lips were in no language Jennie had ever before heard.

"What were you goin' to say?" the cop asked.

"Nothing," Jennie whispered. "I'm so upset I didn't know what I was saying." Inside of her she was telling herself she had changed her mind because all of a sudden she had realized that no one would believe what she had wanted to say, but she knew she was lying. "Let me go. I've got to get back to work. I've lost enough time already."

She had. She must get back to work. Even though she was sick, and all mixed up, and—*afraid*—she had to get back to her machine in the window.

CHAPTER THREE

The Black Sticks' Message

THE crowd melted after the morgue wagon came and took away Maria and what was left of baby Andros. The truck drove off. A street cleaner pitched the jumble of smashed wood that had been a baby carriage into his wheeled garbage can, and then used a hose to wash the cobbles and the sidewalk clean.

In a little while Morris Street was the same as always. The peddlers were yelling again. The shawled women were pinching oranges with their gnarled, wise fingers and the kids were playing in the gutter.

The sun didn't make any more patterns on the pushcarts. It was getting late and the little bit of sky Jennie could see was clouding over.

Jennie couldn't stop thinking about what had happened. When she closed her eyes she could see the terror in Maria's face, and she could feel the black sticks in her hand so distinctly that she could count them. There had been ten of them, and they had been tied together with a ribbon of grey fur.

There must have been some reason for the way they had been snatched from her.

Jennie had no idea what they meant, and the cops would have laughed at her if she had told them her hunch that they had something to do with Maria's killing Andros. But—Jennie's heart started beating faster as she worked it out—but if more things happened to others around here and more sticks were found, then they might be a clue to whoever was behind what was happening.

That was the answer! Maria's baby was not the only one threatened with something so awful she had thought death was better! The terror had not ended, it had only begun.

If that were so, Jennie should have told the cop about the sticks in spite of what Papa Anton had said. Now it was too late.

But something ought to be done about it. Jennie's head was in a whirl. She didn't know what to do.

"Why don't you stop with them stockin's?" Izzy Horowitz said. "Don't yuh know it's quittin' time?"

IT began to drizzle as Jennie hurried along Morris Street toward Cherry Avenue and home. She was worried about Dick, wondering if he'd have sense enough to close the windows. He'd been a little feverish that morning. His nose had been running, and she'd told him to stay in that flat. She had asked Sonia Gorgio, across the hall, to go in once in a while and see how he was, but Sonia had five kids of her own. She might have forgotten and Dickie might be very sick by now.

Cherry Avenue, when Jennie reached and turned into it, was like some place she had never seen before. There was hardly anyone in the street, and the few who were hurried as if anxious to be between four walls.

Even though it was raining, there should have been children running about, the children of the Sylvanians who had made these tenement-lined blocks their own, except for two or three families like the

Gants who lived here before the heavy-bodied, round-headed foreigners came. But there were none at all.

The lights of the street lamps seemed to be closed in under their shades by the dismal dark, so that the shadows between them were blacker than they had ever been.

Something seemed to be creeping after Jennie in the shadows behind her. She told herself there was nothing there, but she was afraid to turn and make sure.

She crossed the street and saw, in the middle of the next block, light streaming out from Otto Erlauber's stationery and candy store that was on the ground floor of the house where Jennie lived. Her apartment was on the top floor.

"That's it!", Jennie said aloud. "Mr. Erlauber will know what I ought to do about the sticks. I'll stop and ask him, right now."

She should have thought of the old German before. He knew everything except how to make money. And he was her friend. Every night she went down to the back room behind his store, and he'd teach her the things she ought to know if she was to be a good wife for Bob when he became a doctor. He had rigged up an electric bell from upstairs so Dickie could call her.

There he was, leaning on the imitation marble counter across the open front of the store, looking out under his dripping awning into the rain.

"Ach!", he exclaimed as Jennie came past the newspaper stand and up to the counter. "Chennie! It is nice that you stop to say good evening to a lonely old man." He peered at her through his thick spectacles. "But is it that you do nod feel so goot? In your cheeks the roses are faded, and your smile—where iss it?" He could speak perfect English, but liked to amuse Jennie with those Germanisms, till they had become a habit.

The light made his white hair silky. It beat down on his great head, bringing out with every fine line of the thousands that netted his face and puckered the corners of his twinkling kindly eyes.

"Mr. Erlauber," Jennie gasped. "You know Maria Leventich from the second floor front? She stopped at my window this afternoon and when she started to lift up baby Andros, he was holding. . . ."

She stopped, with a scary feeling that there was someone behind her, that there were eyes on her. Her head jerked around.

Papa Anton was behind her, looking over the top of a newspaper he held in front of him as if he were reading. His black, fierce eyes, burned into Jennie's brain.

In the next second they were hidden by the newspaper, but Jennie Gant knew that they were there. She dared not say anything more to Mr. Erlauber while the tall black priest was listening.

JENNIE never knew what the words were that rasped from her dry throat, or whether the sound made words at all. She turned and almost ran out from under the awning and into the fine, chill drizzle again.

She didn't go up the stoop next to the candy store and into the house on whose top floor Dickie was waiting for her, because even then she remembered that she needed milk and bread and a can of beans for supper, and that she would never be able to climb those five long flights again. She ran down the block to Zbick's grocery on the far corner and as she ran she could feel the tall, black priest's eyes following her.

There were four of the stocky, blue-eyed Sylvanian women in the grocery when Jennie came into it. Mr. Zbick was waiting on one of them, but the others had been whispering in the middle of the store, their shawled heads close together.

The minute Jennie opened the door they went silent, drawing away from each other, their round flat faces suddenly blank. It was as if a veil had dropped over their faces, over their pale blue eyes. But the veil couldn't hide the fear that lay deep in those eyes.

The woman at the counter, it was Rivcha Chesmy, had a red-headed little girl in her arms, hugged her close to her body.

Jennie had to wait a long time till it was her turn to be waited on. It seemed hours before Mr. Zbick had wrapped her loaf of bread and her can of beans and was dipping a pint of milk into the can she had left with him in the morning.

Mr. Zbick marked how much Jennie owed in the notebook she fished out of her bag, adding the small sum to the other small sums that she would pay on Saturday. Then she was out in the street again.

Papa Anton was no longer beside the newspaper stand, but Mr. Erlauber was selling three cigarettes to a man whose wet overcoat was hunched up about his collarless neck and Jennie was in a hurry now to get to Dickie so she didn't stop.

She went up the stoop into the tenement hallway. Usually the hall was noisy with the shrill voices of women, the guttural ones of men, the laughter of children, coming through thin walls of the flats and their thin doors from which the paint peeled in the little brown flakes. Tonight there was hardly any sound at all, only a low rumble of voices, and from the second floor the cry of a sick baby.

Somewhere ahead Jennie heard the patter of little feet, climbing the stairs in front of her.

There was something queer about the sound of those feet, and it set little prickles chasing each other up and down Jennie's backbone. It was a little scrape, scrape,

scrape, like claws would make on the worn wood of the steps.

The very hall, so strangely hushed, was afraid.

That was silly, Jennie told herself. She was nervous because she was so tired, because of what had happened in front of the laundry.

But when the stairs ended at the top floor there was no one there, and Jennie had not heard a door squeak open and closed on this last landing.

Then it must have been a rat in the walls. The Lord knew there were enough of them in the house. Of course it was a rat. . . .

JENNIE'S key rattled in the keyhole of her door, her hand shook so.

"Hello, Dickie dear, how do you feel?"

"A'right."

His little head, curly as Jennie's own, but blonde as hers was dark, was bent in absorption over something with which his little hands were fussing. "Looka the Injun wigwam I just made."

"Look at the mess you've made," Jennie snapped, her tone sharper than she means because of her exasperation at the nonchalant way he accepted her coming home. "Newspaper cut up all over the floor. And you've been using my manicure scissors, you bad boy." Putting down her bag and the package and the milk can on the rectangular, unpainted table in the middle of the room, she went toward the youngster. "Has your nose been running? Have you coughed any?"

"No. Ain't this a swell tepee?" He lifted it to her, blue eyes dancing in his pinched, pale face; the hole where a front tooth was missing making his grin impish.

"Isn't," Jennie corrected mechanically. Then her heart bumped against her ribs. An iron band squeezed her forehead, and her eyes were so wide they hurt, staring at the thing Dickie held up to her.

It was a small cone of newspaper neatly pinned around a framework of sticks whose ends stuck out through the top, where they were tied by a piece of string. The miniature tepee was about twice the height of a wooden match. *The stick-ends were the thickness of matches, and they were black!*

The sticks out of which Dickie had built his wigwam were exactly like the sticks in the fur-tied bundle that had been the last toy with which baby Andros ever played!

Jennie took the little tent from Dickie. "How—where did you get these sticks?" It was hard to talk. But then, it was harder to think, with her brain going around in a whirl. "Who gave them to you?"

"Nobody gave them to me. I foun' 'em on the floor, just a little while ago, over near the window. They was tied with a little piece of fur." The boy rustled the papers, pushing them aside to look for it.

Jennie had swept up before going to work, and there certainly had been nothing like that on the floor then. The fire-escape platform was outside of that window, but the window was closed and locked, and Dickie could not reach the lock.

"Who was here today? Who came in here?"

"Nobody." Dick was on his hands and knees now, still looking. "Only Mis' Gorgio when she come in to gimmie lunch, an' Uncle Bob."

The boy chuckled. "Was he surprised when I opened the door and yelled 'hello doctor' afore he got halfway up the last stairs."

"How did you know it was him?" Jennie asked, glad to have something to talk about while she tried to pull herself together.

"Gee, that was easy. You know how

he walks, gimpy like. You can know it's him comin' a mile off."

Bob dragged his left leg a trifle because his knee was stiff from something that had happened to it, playing football on Morris Street when he was a kid.

"You're sure no one was here except Mrs. Gorgio and Bob?" Impossible that either had brought the sticks into the flat. But how then. . . .?

"Sure I'm sure. . . . Here's the fur, Jennie." Dick jumped to his feet and pushed it into Jennie's cold fingers.

The hair was grey. It was stiff and coarse, coarser than the hair of any cat's, any dog's, Jennie had ever known. The inside was bluish-white, like Maria's lips had been. . . .

There was a word printed in indelible pencil on the inside of the fur. One word. *"Silence."*

"What's the matter, Jennie?" Dickie's voice was scared all of a sudden. "Why are your eyes so big and black? Why is your mouth so funny? What's the matter?"

"Nothing's the matter, hon. Nothing at all. I was—I was just trying to stop a sneeze."

There was nothing to get scared about. These sticks didn't mean the same thing the other bundle had meant. There were only five, not ten, and the word on the inside of the fur told the message they brought.

If Jennie kept mum about what she had seen that afternoon Dickie would be all right. If she didn't. . . .

What would have happened to Dickie if Papa Anton had heard her finish talking to Mr. Erlauber? In God's name what would she have found here?

She didn't know and she didn't want to know. Wild horses wouldn't drag another word about Maria out of her. . . . Jennie was surprised to find that she had both her arms around Dickie, hugging him

close to her. That she was kissing him fiercely, greedily—the way Maria had kissed her baby just before she had—had thrust its perambulator in the way of a hurtling truck. . . .

CHAPTER FOUR

The Night of Fear

THE little body in Jennie Gant's arms squirmed, pulling away from her. "I'm hungry," Dickie said. "When are we gonna eat?"

Jennie made supper and served it somehow, managed to eat a little though the stuff tasted like hay and stuck in her throat, going down. She managed somehow to smile at Dickie, to get him undressed and washed, to hear him say his prayers and tuck him into his little bed in the living room.

Her feet stumbled as she started inside to her bedroom.

"Where are you goin', Jennie?" Dickie asked sleepily from the bed. "Ain't you goin' down to Mr. Erlauber's?"

"No. I'm tired. I'm too tired."

The boy sat up. "But you must," he cried. "'Member, you made me promise to make you, no matter how tired you are, like you make me go to school no matter how much I don't want to."

"Tonight's different, hon. I'm not going tonight."

"Then the next time I don't want to go to school that will be different too, an' *I* won't go."

She couldn't answer that. She couldn't tell Dickie why she didn't want to leave him alone tonight, and she couldn't think of a good lie. She never lied to him. And why shouldn't she go. He would be all right, as long as she obeyed the warning of the sticks.

"All right," Jennie gave in. "I'll go. But be sure to push the bell button right next to you in the wall if you want me for anything. You will push it right away, won't you?"

"Of course I will, Jennie. G'night, big sister."

"Good night, little brother."

Jennie made sure all the windows in the flat were locked before she turned out the light and went out into the hall. She made sure the door was locked.

She looked down the stairs, down into the dim silent well of the stairs. It was so far down to Mr. Erlauber's store. She would be so terribly far away from Dickie if he rang the bell. And suppose he didn't get a chance to ring it?

But the walls were thin and every sound in her flat could be heard in the Gorgios'. She would ask them to keep an ear out for Dickie. Jennie knocked on the streaked door next to her own.

Feet shuffled inside it. "Who there?"

The man's voice sounded scared through the wood. Awfully scared. "It's Jennie, Mr. Gorgio. Jennie Gant. I want to ask you something."

"Jus' a meenit." Jennie heard the sound of something heavy being shoved away from the door, like some heavy piece of furniture had been holding it closed. The lock clicked, and the door opened.

It didn't open very far, only just enough so that she could see Pavel Gorgio's bristled chin, and a slice of wool undershirt, and it stayed that way, as if Gorgio was ready to slam it shut again any second.

"W'at you want?", his thick voice rumbled.

"I'm going downstairs for a while and I wanted to ask you to listen for any sound from my flat. Sonia has a key so you can go right in."

"You go down alla time. Why you no ask that before? Why you only ask that tonight?"

"I—I'm nervous tonight. I—I'm afraid something might happen to Dickie."

"Afraid." The door moved a little, so that the light from inside fell on the man's hand. A big hand it was, stubby-nailed, black grime of the earth he dug worked into its cracks and seams so that they could never be scrubbed out.

"What do you. . . .?" A yowl—the yelping howl of some enraged beast—cut across Jennie's question. A woman's scream shrill with pain and terror, joined it. They exploded into hideous snarls, yelps. Frightened children screamed from inside the flat.

PAVEL GORGIO was no longer blocking the entrance. Jennie batted the door open with her shoulder, ran after his burly, running form into the kitchen of the flat, through it into a bedroom beyond.

She saw a huddle of screaming kids on a huge bed, saw a woman, Sonia Gorgio,

---

FESTIVAL OF THE BLOODLESS DEAD

In brilliant, colored lights and garish trappings terror came to Lacey Street. Yet when the dreadful festival was over, Robert Rodman knew the horror was there to stay; for the bloodless dead were found each night—and his own sweetheart had been marked as one who must quench with her blood the ghastly thirst that walked abroad!

In Weird-Menace # 2. $5 a copy.

at an open window beyond them. Sonia's mouth was open, but the scream was no longer coming from it. Scarlet streaks gashed her face, her wrinkled brown breast from which the kimono hung in shreds. The rags of a torn sleeve fluttered from her arm and on its flabby round there were the red marks of small teeth that had sunk deep.

"Sonia" Pavel grunted plunging to her. "W'at. . . ."

"Carlo. He ees taken. I could not hold heem. Look." She twisted that bitten arm of hers thrusting out through the window pointing through it.

Jennie reached them as the man vented guttural exclamation; oath and heart-wrung groan in one sound. She leaned out of the window with them, her body crushed between theirs.

The iron bars of a firescape platform, the same upon which Jennie's own window opened slatted across her vision. But through them, on a far down slant of the wet-gleaming iron ladder she saw a small dark form descending. Small—it was Carlo the four-year-old youngest of the Gorgio brood, in his grey wool nightie.

He wasn't *climbing* down the ladder! He was underneath it, slinging himself down by arms and oddly prehensile legs on the ladder's underside, and he was mewling and spitting and snarling like nothing that had ever been human.

Below him, blacker in the blackness of the backyard, a shapeless thing moved to the foot of the ladder. Carlo dropped into that formless shadow. . . .

Shadow—and Carlo—melted together into black. Jennie realized the others were no longer on each side of her. 'Eet ees your fault," Pavel Gorgio's hoarse bellow pulled her back into the room. "You were too steenky to pay. Your fault. . . ." His arm was upraised, the sledge-hammer fist at its end knotted to strike his wife.

Something in Sonia's pose, rigid,

poignantly tragic, stayed that blow. "Steengy? Yes. For these othairs. Steengy weet' the money that mus' buy food for *their bellies*." She pointed to the four whimpering, trembling little girls on the big bed. "An' I had faith in the cross."

Jennie saw it, the strange black cross of the Sylvanian's strange sect, shattered on the floor. And atop the fragments, as if for all its light weight it had smashed the cross, she saw a fagot of ten black sticks bound together by a scrap of grey fur!

"WHAT is it, Sonia? What is this night? What is happening?"

"Jennie!" The woman, bleeding, distraught, looked at her as if for the first time. "Thees ees not your affair. Get out."

"But. . . ."

"Get out." Sonia pushed at Jennie with furious strength, pushed her past the heavy table that had been against the door, pushed her out into the hall. The door slammed.

The walls whirled dizzily around Jennie. She swayed, clutched at the banister for support. She didn't know what to do.

"They are bewildered aliens in this strange land. They are prey to the exploiters of their new country and to the superstitions of their old. Who can live among them and not pity them, and not desire to help them?"

Mr. Erlauber had said that once, when Jennie had asked him why he spent so much of his time talking to the dumb, stupid Sylvanians, so much time advising them. "Even against their will, their wish, it is our duty to help them whenever we can." If anyone could help the Gorgios, Mr. Erlauber could.

Jennie slipped, flinging herself around the turn of a landing. Her hand, pawing at the wall to save her from falling, ripped away a length of bellwire that was tacked to it. She gasped, her heart jumping in her throat, stopped and flung herself around to it. It was the wire from the push button beside Dickie's bed to the bell in the room behind Mr. Erlauber's store. If she had broken it . . . !

She hadn't. She had only pulled out one of the staples that held it.

Jennie started running down again, but what had happened reminded her of Dickie, and she was again afraid for him in spite of what Pavel Gorgio had said. She would tell Mr. Erlauber about what was happening as quick as she could, and run right back upstairs.

Her feet hit the bottom landing and she darted around under the slant of the stairs to where one door led to the cellar stairs and another, at right angles to it, to Mr. Erlauber's back room. She knocked at this second door.

He didn't open. Maybe he was out in the store, waiting on someone. Jennie didn't care. She knocked again, rattled the doorknob. Still her old friend didn't come to open it.

Had something happened to him too? Jennie leaned against the door, putting he rear close to it, trying to listen through it. She heard only the throb throb, of the blood in her own ear. . . .

Suddenly fingers clutched her arm, digging in, twisting her around. A scream started in her chest. . . .

"Ach, it's Chennie!" Mr. Erlauber exclaimed. "I thought. . . ." Behind him, a grotesque silhouette against the pale rectangle of the cellar door, open now, was Joe, the hunchbacked half-wit janitor.

Joe had a bucket of coal on his shoulder. Jennie understood that Mr. Erlauber had gone down to the basement for coal for the stove that kept his store warm and that Joe was carrying it up for him.

"You are trembling, Chennie," the old German was saying as he peered into her face through his thick lenses. "Something the matter is, hah? The little Dick. . . ."

"No. Dickie is all right. It's Carlo Gorgio. . . ." Jennie checked herself as Joe's apelike head jerked toward her, its thick lips drooling, its eyes red-balled and bleary. "No. Nothing's the matter. I just came down for my lesson and I was running because I was late."

Mr. Erlauber's face showed that he understood she didn't want Joe to hear what she had to say. "So let us go in and begin." He stuck his key into the door and unlocked it.

THEY all went in to the room where Mr. Erlauber lived, and Jennie stood looking around her while Joe shambled past and out through a curtained doorway into the store. It was a little room, but it was neat as a pin. Two of its walls were covered with shelves full of books, all the way up to the ceiling, and more books were piled against a third wall, handy to a cot whose blankets were folded at its foot in a square whose edges looked as though they had been sliced with a knife.

In the middle of the room was a desk with a green-shaded lamp on it, and papers covered with writing in little angular letters as clean-cut as if they had been engraved. Another table against the fourth wall held a two-burner gas-plate. Above the table were more shelves with neat rows of shining pots and dishes, and boxes and cans of food. Next to it was a sink and a small icebox.

Joe came back. He lumbered past her, his crooked body almost as wide as it was high, his arms hanging down almost to his knees, his hands black with coal and curled like a Gorilla's.

Mr. Erlauber closed the hall door behind Joe. Then he turned to Jennie.

"Well? What is it dot troubles my Chennie?"

She told him, the words tumbling out from between her lips, about Maria and about the sticks out of which Dickie had made a wigwam; and about the Gorgios. He listened, his face getting graver, his blue eyes darker behind the glasses that made them twice as big as they should be. He nodded when Jennie described the sticks, and when she was getting to the end he plodded over and lifted a big book down from one of the shelves and took it over to the desk.

"It can't be true," Jennie cried, as she finished, "what Maria said! Satan isn't real, is he? He isn't here in Morris Street?"

The book fell open to a page about in the middle. "Never, my dear Chennie, say dot anything cannod be true. One thing I have learned in my long years of study and wandering, dot the more science man learns, the less he knows about the eternal verities. Science muddies the waters of truth. . . ."

"You mean. . . ?"

"I mean dot belief, call it religion or superstition, makes true whatever is believed. When five hundred million people belief dot bread and wine may be transformed by faith into the flesh and blood of their God, then it is true as dot water can by an electric current be transformed into a gas. When five hundred people belief dot on one certain night of the year Satan is free to roam even this mechanistic city and change their children into hounds of hell, den all your science cannod deny it."

"But. . . ."

"Dese old eyes have beheld things incredible, my Chennie. Once in the Transvaal, I recollect, an eland pale like a corpse long dead. . . ." He cut off, stopped by a tinkle from the store that told someone was opening the door. He sighed, pushed out through the curtain.

JENNIE heard the door slam closed. She heard footfalls come across the floor; rap, scuff, rap, scuff. Bob's footfalls, unmistakable! She pushed the curtain aside to call to him.

Her lover was picking up a box of cough drops from the counter, shoving a nickel across to Mr. Erlauber. She saw his long, narrow student's face, his high forehead and dark, tired eyes. But she did not call his name. . . . There was someone else in the store. A tall man, black-gowned, black-bearded, black-hatted!

Had Papa Anton come in with Bob or had he been out there all the time, overhearing what Jennie had said to Mr. Erlauber?

Jennie must have made some sound, because Bob turned and saw her. "Jen!" he exclaimed. "Sweetheart!" and then his smile of gladness faded. "What's the matter, hon? You look sick." He was limping toward her, his face anxious. "You look—terrified."

The black priest's eyes were on Jennie, orbs of black fire in an ominous face. "I'm just tired, Bob." She could lie to him once, but if she asked her another question she could not lie again, and Papa Anton would hear her. "But you're due at the warehouse. You mustn't stop here talking. If you're late again you'll be fired."

"Gosh," Bob said, looking at the clock on the wall. "That's right. But. . . ."

"Hurry, Bob."

"Night, sweetheart." He was turning. He was going to the door. Jennie let the curtain fall between her and Papa Anton's terrible look. Her legs were weak, so that she had to put her hands on the desk to hold herself up. One of them touched the book. She looked at it, trying to tell herself that there was no real reason for her to be afraid of Papa Anton.

The book was open to a picture, yellowed with age. The scene was a clearing in a forest. The devil was coming out of a big hole in the ground. In front of him was a woman holding a baby in one arm while her other hand held out a necklace of pearls to the devil.

Behind the woman there was a child that was like a dog from the waist down, and another that had the head of a dog on a little boy's naked body. A man was running away through the trees, and the thing that ran after him was a dog, except that its forelegs were human arms and hands, and the shaggy hind legs had human feet.

A bundle of black sticks. . . . A bell over Jennie's head started ringing, its shrill sound piercing her ears, stabbing her breast. *Dickie's bell!* The way it rang was as if Dickie was screaming to her, screaming for help.

Jennie flew out of the door into the hall, threw herself at the stairs. The bell stopped ringing, all of a sudden.

That was more terrible than if it had kept on.

CHAPTER FIVE

Punishment

SOME time must have gone by between when Jennie heard the bell and started up the stairs, and when she reached the top floor—but she didn't remember any of it. It seemed that one second she was in Mr. Erlauber's room and the next she was holding on to the knob of her flat door with one hand while with the other she was trying to get her key into the keyhole.

"Dickie!" she yelled. "Dick."

There wasn't any answer. There wasn't any sound at all from the other side of the door. *"Dickie!"*

The key rattled in the lock against a background of awful silence.

The key caught, turned over. *"Dick."*

The blackness inside took Jennie's scream and smothered it. She thumbed the switch beside the door jamb and the room jumped into being.

Dickie wasn't in his bed. He wasn't anywhere in the room. Jennie ran into the bathroom, whimpering. "Dickie. Dickie." She ran in and out of the kitchen, in and out of her own room, knowing she wouldn't find him, hoping against hope that she would.

She did not. The little boy was nowhere in the flat.

But the door had been locked and he didn't have a key to lock it from outside.

Maybe he had slid down under the bedcovers. Jennie ran back into the front room, grabbed the blankets and pulled them loose.

The blankets were still warm, the sheets were dented where his little body had lain. In the depression a bundle of black sticks lay, tied together by a scrap of grey fur. A bundle of *ten* black sticks. Not a warning. A sign of what had happened to her little brother. A sign that Jennie was being punished for having talked out of turn after the five sticks had warned her not to.

Jennie stared at the black fagot, and it was as if she were having a nightmare. The inside of her was filled with a terrible fear. She couldn't move and she couldn't make a sound.

Not that it would do her any good to scream. She had screamed before, with the door open, and no one had come.

They had sense enough to be afraid. *They* had sense enough to keep mum about that which it was forbidden to talk. *They* would not destroy their loved ones with their tongues, as Jennie had done.

What was happening to Dick? For what awful purpose had he been taken?

The weight of the blankets pulled them out of Jennie's numbed hand, pulled them off the bed. They uncovered another tiny bundle of sticks.

There were only five in this bundle, and the ribbon of grey fur that tied them together also tied a piece of paper to them. There were words printed on the paper, in indelible pencil. Jennie read the words.

> You cannot help him. Attempt it and the earth will engulf you too in enternal agony. Do nothing, say nothing or the doom of Satan's night overtakes you.

THE words traced themselves in letters of fire on Jennie's soul, and then they were fading, were gone! There was only the blank paper, tied to the sticks. But their meaning. . . .

Cold lashed Jennie's cheek, cold rain whipped against her cheek by a cold wind. It twisted her to the window. The wide open window! She had left it locked.

Jennie started for the window. A pair nail scissors, the ones with which Dick had cut the newspaper, were on the table. She snatched them up, and then she was leaning out of the window, her aching eyes straining through the slatted grid of the firescape platform, probing the rain-filled darkness.

She was just in time to glimpse, far down, a small dark form descending the last iron rungs of the last ladder. Dickie! Who else could it be? A shapeless shadow received him and flowed away into the glistening darkness of the backyard.

Jennie shoved the scissors into the pocket of her skirt. Her knees thumped the sill, shoving her through the window, out on the firescape.

A panic gibbered at her, terror froze her motionless on her knees. Once before she had received a warning and ignored it. If she ignored this one. . . .

Dickie was down there, the little brother she loved, the tot she had prom-ised her dying mother to cherish and protect! Jennie came upright on the iron slats of the firescape. Then her feet were on the slippery wet rungs of the ladder, and she was going down, so fast that it seemed as though the far-down yard were pulling her down to it, down to her doom.

Water on the broken concrete splashed icily on her ankles. Jennie peered about her in the gloom, garbage smell in her nostrils, fear tightening her throat. The rain sifted down on her, soaked into her clothes, pasted them cold and wet against her skin. But it was not from the cold that she shuddered.

The stinking dark filled the yard—Darker still, a shadow lay against the black loom of the broken fence. Dickie must be in that shadow, a part of it. It was moving, going away from her! Taking Dickie. . . . Jennie sobbed, threw herself at the shadow to fight it, to tear Dickie away from it before it got away.

The ground vanished under her feet. She dropped into abysmal blackness!

The earth had opened to engulf her! A scream tore Jennie's throat, was smashed back into it as she smashed down on hardness that crashed the black into her skull.

SOMETHING pricked Jennie's thigh. A sharp point stung her arm. She struck at it, waking from the oblivion that momentarily had claimed her. Something squealed in the dark. Tiny feet scuttered away, claws scraping on stone.

Jennie's eyes opened to darkness. If she had thought the night black before, then what could she call this velvet ebony that lay against her eyes like something palpable.

Jennie's stomach knotted. Her head ached where she had hit it, and inside it there was a dizzy whirl. She shoved her hands against slimy stone on which she lay, pushing herself up to a sitting posture.

All around her she heard the scuttering, scraping sounds of uncountable small things. She pulled in a breath, pulled in with it a smell of rottenness, a stench of things foul when alive and now dead for a long, long time.

A green spark lit up in the blackness, another, close to it. Two more, and two more, appeared, and then there were hundreds of the twin green lights all about Jennie in the dark. *They were eyes!* They were eyes watching her, hating her!

Fur rubbed against stone. Something squealed. Jennie knew that squeal. She had heard it before, in the wall of the tenement.

Jennie know now what it was that had nipped her to consciousness. She knew now whose eyes it was that watched her out of the dark, waiting for her to stop moving, waiting to leap on her and tear her flesh with sharp teeth. *Rats!* Hundreds, thousands of rats.

Jennie jumped up, her skin crawling with the imagined feel of the rats. The rats' eyes blinked out. The scutter of their running feet was like the patter of a storm on the roof. But they did not run far. The green sparks of their eyes blinked into being again, not far away. They watched her. They knew she couldn't get away from them. They knew they would have her if they waited long enough. And they were waiting.

"Lemme go. I. . . ."

It was Dick's voice, far away and muffled at once as though a hand had been clapped across his mouth, but unmistakably the voice of her little brother. You couldn't fool Jennie about that.

JENNIE forgot the rats. She was listening for the voice again, for Dickie's voice. She didn't hear it again, but she did hear the sound of someone moving, very far away. The thud of heavy feet, of feet that scuffed on stone, far away and getting farther.

Jennie started running. Right at the rats she ran, forgetting her fear of them, forgetting everything except that she had heard her little brother's voice, that he was somewhere there ahead of her, and that she must get to him.

Slipping once, she was thrown against the wall, and it was round and greasy with rotten slime. She was running a little downhill, and all of a sudden her feet were splashing in water; in greasy, oily water that splashed on her ankles and stuck to them, running off from them only slowly, so thick it was with rot.

Once more Jennie slipped. The thick, stinking water splashed into her face. . . . Her feet couldn't find the stone floor! She was in a bottomless pool of the soupy water!

Jennie went crazy altogether when she realized that. She couldn't swim and she had been always afraid of drowning, and she was going to drown in this awful stuff. She fought it, wildly, frantically, hitting it with her threshing arms, her flailing legs, and the more she fought it the more it splashed into her mouth and her nose, cutting off her breath, choking her.

She had sense enough not to breathe in the poisonous stuff, making her throat tight against it, against her screams. But she couldn't stand it any longer. Knives were cutting her lungs, blackness was throbbing in her skull. She was going to die!

Dickie. . . .

Hands grabbed Jennie under the armpits, dragging at her. Her head came free of the water. Breath gusted into her face, breath that was hot and foul. Her face was shoved against the body of her rescuer and filthy hair matting that body scratched her face, got into her mouth. This was no human being that was lifting her out of the pool where she had almost drowned. It was an animal. . . .

Was it a huge rat, huge as a man, that was saving her from drowning? Vaguely Jennie knew that that couldn't be so, and then she didn't know anything any more.

CHAPTER SIX

Santan's Prison

JENNIE GANT was cold. Her whole body hurt, terribly, every little bit of it. Maybe she had the flu. Maybe she had caught it from Dickie.

Dickie. Something had happened to him. Something. . . . Jennie had been having a nightmare. Something about black sticks, and the devil, and rats in a sewer. . . .

What. . . ? It was a wooden ceiling Jennie's head had bumped against, close over her head. The black stripes were rusty iron bars, framed in a panel, hinged and held closed by a big padlock. Jennie was in a cage!

The cage was so small that there was just about enough room for her to lie outstretched. A blue light came from a fire down there in the middle of a stone floor that was about three feet below the bottom of the cage.

It was a bundle of sticks that burned with that strange blue flame. a bundle of black sticks! They were bigger, each about the size of Dickie's baseball bat, but otherwise they were exactly like the sticks in the little fagots she had been seeing all day.

The blue light reached out from the blue fire and flickered on rows of big stone pillars, streaked with damp and black with age, whose tops joined in stone arches on which a stone ceiling was laid. The blue light reached behind the pillars and danced on tiers of iron-barred cages like the one in which Jennie was.

The cages were like shelved bins piled on top of one another. And there was movement inside them.

Jennie became conscious of small sounds in the room. Maybe they had been too small to hear before. Maybe her hearing had come back more slowly than her sight. But she heard the sounds now.

They were the pad, pad of small soft feet. They were the whimpering of small animals. They were a low moan.

The fire flared higher. The blue light was brighter, bright enough to reach into the cages, bright enough to show Jennie what moved in the cages.

There was a grey dog in one of them, loping back and forth, back and forth. In the next another small form prowled back and forth. But this wasn't a dog. This was a little boy.

It was Carlo Gorgio!

The fire died down again just as Jennie saw Carlo, and she could not be sure, but it seemed to her that his little arms and his little legs were black and shaggy, as if they had fur on them.

When the fire flared up again Jennie wasn't looking at that cage. Her face was shoved against the bars in front of her and she was looking at others.

There were children in some of them and there were dogs in others. Jennie didn't look long at any one of the cages. Her staring eyes were going along the long tiers, faster and faster.

She was looking for Dickie.

Her eyes went along the cages and reached the stone wall at the end of the room, and she hadn't found Dick. She stared at the wall, and at the high, wide door in it that was stuck full of rusted rivet-heads and bound with rusted iron straps, and she was trying not to hear the voice that was whispering inside of her skull.

"You've seen him but you didn't know him," the voice was whispering. "Remember the picture in Mr. Erlauber's book? Dick is like that now. *He has been changed into a dog!*"

JENNIE'S hands closed on the bars of her cage, and she tried to tear them apart. They didn't move, but the rust on them cut into her palms, tearing her skin. The pain of that ran up Jennie's arms to her brain and it silenced the whispering voice, clearing her brain.

She hadn't seen all of the cages. Some of them were on her side of the room and some of them were behind pillars so that she could not see into them. Maybe Dickie was in one of those. Maybe if she called to him. . . ?

Then a scream ripped out—not exactly a scream. It was the shriek of that great door's rusted hinges, and the door was swinging open.

It might be a scene out of hell itself that was framed by that stone arch. Within a semi-circle of blazing fagots an appalling

apparition stood, red cloaked, red hooded, red hand upraised. Before him a waist-high platform was swathed in red draperies and past that, past the curve of the blue fires, Jennie saw a cluster of people who seemed to have been about to surge forward and been stopped by that threatening hand.

She made out men and women there, all of them rigid, all held motionless as if by the paralysis of a nightmare, their faces ghastly with the blue light upon them and ghastlier still with a strange mixture of blind wrath and blind terror. Beyond them the wavering light was swallowed by darkness into which Jennie sensed space stretching endlessly away.

The door swung wide, showing the person who had opened it. This one, too, was cloaked and hooded, but in dull black. Grotesquely misshapen, he seemed the shadow of some delirium that had taken material form to serve as Satan's acolyte.

"You are those who have defied me because you have come far from the forests of the Ob and have forgotten the power that is mine this night." The black figure moved into the room and passed out of Jennie's sight behind a pillar. A key scraped in a rusty padlock. "I shall prove to you that I still have that power." The devil's disciple came into sight again going out through the doorway. His back was to Jennie, but it seemed to her that he was carrying something. "Before your eyes I shall prove it."

He moved aside. Jennie saw what was on the altar. She saw a small boy's form, bound hand and foot, and gagged. She saw a small head capped by blonde, clustering curls.

She had found Dickie!

Before the scream that tore at Jennie's chest could tear free, before her bleeding hands could begin to shake the bars they still clutched, Satan's arm swept out in a circling gesture above the dais. The fiery arc exploded in a sheet of blue flame, blinding her, blinding all human eyes in that cave of hell.

The glare filled the cavern and was gone. Then indeed a high, shrill shriek ripped from Jennie's throat, a scream of anguish that cut her larynx with its knife-edge. But it was only one thin thread in the pandemonium of the mad dog's howling, of the screams of those others who had witnessed that incredible thing.

On the red bed of Satan's altar a small, bound thing writhed in agony. Not Dickie. *It was a dog,* a yellow-furred little dog from whose bandaged jaws the foam of madness frothed.

CHAPTER SEVEN

Death's White Fangs

ABOVE the screams and the dogs' howling and the deafening clangor of the cage doors at which the dogs plunged, a triumphant laugh boomed out, hollow and humorless and gloating. It was Satan who laughed, but it was his grotesque acolyte who lifted the little yellow dog, its jaws still bound, and shambled with it into this inner chamber.

Jennie saw the gaunt small form twist, hanging from gross hands by the scruff of its neck, and then the pillar hid it.

"Dick!" she whispered, robbed of her voice by the screams that had torn her throat to ribbons. "Oh Dickie." Her hands slipped from the bars, exhaustion numbing them, as the black being reappeared, shambled out through the great door and tugged it shut upon sight and sound beyond it.

Jennie lay whimpering on the floor of her cage, her brain no longer working. And suddenly she was very still. Something had stuck her, just below the waist. It was sticking into her now. She knew what it was. The point of the nail scissors she had stuck into a pocket of her skirt and forgotten.

Slowly, stealthily, she fumbled her fingers into that pocket and fumbled the scissors out of them. They were of good strong steel, and the points were narrow. They were narrow enough to poke into the keyhole of the padlock and to work around inside it.

If the padlock was not old and rusted it could not have happened. Even then it needed something else. Luck, maybe. Anyway, the points of the scissors caught on something inside the lock, and there was a click and it sprang open.

Jennie climbed down to the floor, swayed a minute against the wall of cages, and then started moving. She went along between a line of pillars and the cages till she came to the last of the great stone columns, and there she stopped.

The yellow dog lay on its side against the bars of the cage at which she stared, its jaws freed. It saw her and its moaning stopped, but its flanks kept heaving and its eyes were balls of red flame.

"Dickie," Jennie whispered, her hands going to the rusted padlock with the scissors. "Little brother . . . " The padlock clanged against the iron frame. The dog rolled, was on its feet, was leaping at the bars. His hot muzzle struck Jennie's hand and if she had not snatched it away his foam-covered fangs would have sunk into her flesh.

He fell back, haunched, snarling. In that instant Jennie remembered Maria's words, *"I no can buy heem from Satan so I geeve heem back to God."* and they had a new and terrible meaning. Baby Andros was dead and at peace. Dickie was doomed to live on, a dog, a rabid dog!

He sprang! Swift as light Jennie's hand darted through the bars to meet that lunge. The scissors in it plunged into the dog's throat, and ripped . . . .

THE small yellow body pounded down on the cage floor. Blood gushed from the torn throat. Jennie stared at the furry little form that was so still, so dreadfully still. "God take him," she prayed. "God rest him." Then she looked at the bloody scissors in her torn and bleeding hands, and she prayed, "God have mercy on me." Her left hand went to her neck, ripped away the neck of her waist so that there would be nothing to interfere with the steel. Her right hand came up slowly, its fingers gripping the scissors . . . .

"Jennie. Mees Jennie."

The thin, piping call came from a cage on the other side of the chamber. Carlo Gorgio was crowded against its bars, his small hands thrust through them, pleading.

"Take me out from here, Mees Jennie."

Jennie realized what she had been about to do, and hated herself for it. She had thought only of Dickie and herself, that she had killed Dickie and that she wanted nothing more than to follow him to wherever he had gone. She had forgotten that there were other children here, children who had not yet been damned by Satan. She must save them. She would get them out of their cages and somehow she must find a way to get them away.

She went across the stone floor, went past the blue fire . . . A squeal jerked her head around!

It was the rust-frozen hinges of the great door that were squeaking. The door was opening! Thick hairy fingers curled over its edge, the fingers of Satan's assistant. He was coming in for another victim! If he saw her . . . !

Terror twisted in Jennie's breast, roared in her ears. She whirled, saw that the blue glow did not quite reach the other end of the chamber, darted towards it. If she could get to the shadows before the door came fully open, hide there, he might not notice her empty cage.

The hinges screamed as the door moved faster. A blank stone wall rose in front of Jennie. She stopped herself with her hands against it, went down to her knees, cowering in the shadow which was not dark enough to hide her.

She heard the rasp of shambling feet on the stone, moving toward her. He was coming, he had seen her and he was coming for her, slowing, inexorably, sure she could not escape him. The sound stopped!

Jennie made her head turn, made herself look behind her. She saw a black, grotesque form silhouetted against the green-streaked grey of the closed door. The black hood was turning about, hesitant as if the eyes hidden within it were scanning the cages, momentarily uncertain which one to choose. They had not spied her! She was still safe. She still had a chance.

The invisible head nodded in decision and the grotesque body it topped got into motion again. Jennie strained to see which cage it approached, made out within it the russet curls of Marta, the little girl whom she had last seen in Zbick's grocery with Rivcha Chesny's protecting arm around her. Marta was to be the next . . . .

Stones scraped behind Jennie! The noise was terribly loud and the devil's servant heard it He came around to it. He saw Jennie. His bellow of rage filled the chamber and he lurched into a shambling run toward her.

THE fire threw his shadow before him, a grotesque blackness darting ahead of him. It reached her and she screamed, coming up to her feet, her back against the wall. The gigantic figure plunged toward her. The wall was behind her. There was no escape.

A hand grabbed her shoulder, pulled her sidewise and back—back through the wall itself! "Jen!" Someone yelled in her ears. "Get down that ladder, quick!" It was Bob's voice that yelled! It was Bob who had pulled her back with him through an opening in the wall that had not been there a second before. He was filthy with green slime, his face was a pale staring oval in the dimness, and his hand was at the pocket of his mackinaw, pulling at the butt of a gun.

They were on a shelf-like ledge, and behind Bob a circular black pit yawned, the ends of a ladder's uprights jutting out of it.

"Quick!" Bob yelled again, and Jennie went over the edge of the pit.

Then a shadow blotted the blue glow coming through the opening in the wall above. The black fiend's bellow blasted down to her. She looked up.

Bob's hand wrenched at his pocket. Cloth tore and his hand came free with his gun. Too late. A black shape lurched through the hole in the wall, bellowing, smashed into him. The two merged into one swaying mass, up there.

Metal flashed, streaking down to Jennie. Bob's gun hit the ground at her feet. She bent to snatch it up.

Wood smashed. Broken wood of the ladder sliced her arm. A whirling huge mass hurtled down, pounded into her, knocked her down. She slid down a steep, slime-slick slope and behind her there was a roar, cut off by a gigantic splash.

Jennie dug knees, elbows into the stone on which she was sliding, braked herself to a stop. She twisted to look behind her.

Far behind, and above her, a blue radiance one shade better than darkness glowed about a monstrous black blotch crouched beneath the aperture through which it came. From just beyond it came the slow plop, plop of bubbles breaking the surface of a pool thickened to soup by the things that had rotted in it.

Those bubbles came from Bob's lungs. The monster had landed safely and Bob had fallen into the pool. He was drowning there.

Something hard hurt Jennie's palm. It was the gun. She still had it. Her teeth

bit into her lip and she lifted it. There was no grief, no despair in her brain. There was only the thirst for vengeance.

She pulled the trigger. Nothing happened. Nothing at all . . . .

The dark shape moved, up there! He had sensed her! He was coming after her! Panic ran icy through Jennie's veins. She started to jump up . . . Her feet slid out from under her and she pitched down the sharp slope She went straight down, suddenly. Thudded into something soft and cold.

JENNIE fought erect somehow, but there was water about her ankles and mud under the water sucked at her feet. Somehow she got moving, kept on moving.

After a long while it got colder, and a little lighter. Jennie kept on. Sometimes there was mud sucking at her feet, and sometimes there was hard ground, or ground neither hard nor soft, but slippery, so that she fell to her knees. When that happened the black flame of terror leaped high within her, and her arms would flail around till she got hold of something by which to pull herself up.

All of a sudden the black wall wasn't at Jennie's left any longer. There were lights instead, spreading on the surface of a muddy flat that stretched between them and her. Jennie realized that the blackness of terror and despair had seeped somewhat out of her brain. She realized that the lights she saw were the lamps along the cobbled width of Eastern Avenue, the waterfront street that by day was alive with trucks and shouting men, but now was deserted and silent as the grave.

Jennie knew then that she somehow had gotten to the river, that the wall that had loomed above her was the end of a half-block wide wharf. But she did not know how long she had been struggling through the tunnel, and the muck and mire of low tide. She did not know how far she had wandered in a daze that was close to madness.

She still was not thinking very clearly, but she knew dimly that she must get out of the river. She resumed her painful progress, forcing her tired legs to carry her to those lights, dragging herself along the side of the wharf, past whose corner she had come. Just as she got to the wharf's street-end her left hand lost its hold on a broad bollard and she brought over her right to help it. Something hard in her right hand thumped against the wood.

It was a revolver. It was Bob's revolver. Somehow she had held on to it through her daze. This was the gun that had failed her, back there in that fetid tunnel. She started to throw it away—then paused.

There was light here, and she saw why it had misfired. A bit of green slime, something that had not quite rotted away, was tangled in the hammer, had jammed it. Jennie picked it out with trembling fingers, not knowing why she expected yet to have use for this gun.

Then she knew. She heard the melancholy howl of a dog. She had heard that in her delirium, but she had not imagined it. One of Satan's mad dogs was free.

Jennie crouched against the bollard, hidden by its wide girth, and waited for the dog. It howled again, much nearer, and now she heard the patter of its running feet. It was coming toward the river, down the street the corner of which she could just see, and it was coming fast. There was the sound of other feet too, the pounding of heavy feet, of Satan's black servitor of course. He had set the dog on Jennie's trail, was hunting her down.

A WOMAN appeared out of an alley between two of the warehouses that lined the other side of Eastern Avenue. The lights of the corner street lamp took her, and Jennie saw that it was Rivcha Chesney.

Rivcha looked about her and called out, in a plaintive voice. "Marta!" Her voice was husky, as if she had been calling for a long time. "Where are you, Marta?"

The dog's howl was appallingly near.

Jennie's mouth opened to call to the shawled woman, to tell her where her little girl was. But just then the dog howled again, and it came around the corner into the light.

It saw Rivcha Chesney, stopped abruptly, swung around to her. It hunched, growling, its eyes red balls, its fangs dripping foam. The street lamp shed its light on the dog's fur, and it was russet, red as Marta's hair had been.

Rivcha's arms flung out. The dog leaped, its white fangs gleaming, straight for her throat. Then orange-red flame lashed through the dimness, a shot blasted the silence. The dog's body struck the woman's shoulder, jolted from its course, fell to the sidewalk. Writhed there, yelping.

It wasn't Jennie who had shot. She had not dared, she was no marksman. It was a policeman who had pounded around the corner at that last instant.

"Mad dog," the policeman yelled, his face abruptly white. Rivcha was down on her knees on the sidewalk. She was gathering the wounded dog in her arms. "Don't!" The cop yelled. "That dog's mad."

"Eet ees Marta," the woman wailed. "My Marta," and hugged the bleeding, furry body to her breast . . . . The dog's head snapped up. Its teeth drove into Rivcha's throat, clamped shut . . . .

"God!" the cop blurted. "Batty. Batty as a loon."

CHAPTER EIGHT

Satan's Vengeance

OTHER cops crowded around the dead woman and the dead dog. People too, crowded around them, sprung magically out on the deserted street as crowds do in the city when anything happens. Jennie watched them from the concealment of the bollard, watched for a chance to slip past them unnoticed.

She didn't want them to see her. She didn't want them to ask what had happened to her, why she was torn and soaked with the slime of the tunnel and the muck of the river. She had something to do, and she was going to let no one interfere with her.

"Batty," the cop had called Rivcha, who had gathered her dying daughter into her arms. Batty they would call Jennie if she told them about Satan and how he turned children into dogs. But she knew it was true. Dickie was dead, and Bob was dead, and only vengeance was left to Jennie, but that she would have.

She could not find her way back to the tunnel. Its entrance was somewhere along the river front, but she had no idea how far she had come from it. But she had read the street sign on the lamp post, Hogbund Lane, and all of a sudden she knew how she could find the chamber where Satan was.

The dog, Marta, had escaped from there, beyond doubt, and she had run down Hogbund Lane. The Byzantine Church was on Hogbund Lane. Papa Anton's church! Jennie recalled how Papa Anton had stopped her from telling about the sticks that afternoon, how right after he had heard her start to talk to Mr. Erlauber about them, the warning fagots had appeared on the floor of her flat. Papa Anton had been in Mr. Erlauber's store, had heard her tell her story to the old German, and at once after that Dickie's bell had rung and Dickie had been gone.

Maybe Satan let Papa Anton keep the money people would pay to keep him from turning their children into dogs. Hadn't both Maria and Sonia Gorgio said something about buying their kids from the devil? None of the Sylvanians had much,

but there were many of them and a little from each would make a lot of money.

Maybe Papa Anton *was* Satan.

Whatever he was, Jennie had figured out that if she found Papa Anton she would find the key to the mystery. She saw her chance to get across Eastern Avenue unseen. Minutes later she had made her way, keeping in the shadows, up Hogbund Lane to the Byzantine Church, and was crouched in the darkness against its wall, waiting for a peddler to drag his empty pushcart past her along the sidewalk.

She was in the angle between the steps leading up to the wide, high door of the church, and its wall. Ten feet above her a small window was lighted, and its yellow oblong was the only light in the block except for the street lamps.

The wall was of rough-hewn stone. Her toes just could catch in the spaces between them. Any other time Jennie would have been afraid to try climbing that wall, but there wasn't any room in her pounding skull for that kind of fear. There was room only for the idea that had brought her here. She was more than half mad, and surely there was reason enough for that in all she had gone through.

She went up that wall like a cat climbing a backyard fence, using only one hand because the other held the gun. Her knees came up on the wide sill. She peered through the window.

The room she saw was like an office, its walls bare except for a couple of framed pictures on it, a desk in its center. Seated at that desk, his back toward her, was Papa Anton, in his black cassock. Jennie could see his hand. There was something in it — *a tiny bundle of black sticks, bound by a bit of grey fur.*

JENNIE tried the window sash with her free hand. It moved up a little, quite without sound. Her fingers slid in under its lower edge and then, in what seemed like one motion, she had flung the window up and jumped through it into the room. Papa Anton must have heard the thump of her landing, for he jumped up and whirled around, his chair crashing to the floor.

"Keep back," Jennie exclaimed shoving the gun at him. She must have been a weird spectacle, covered from head to foot by slime and river muck. "Keep back or I'll shoot."

"Retro me, Sathanas!" the black priest exclaimed. His hand flailed from behind him, hurled an inkwell at Jennie's head. She dodged it, her gun going off, thunderous.

Papa Anton jolted back against the desk, and then he was sliding down, his black cassock suddenly blacker over his breast with a glistening wetness that spread rapidly. He went down like a ripped doll out of whose body the sawdust was running, and settled limply on the floor. His face got grey, above his black beard and his eyes widened with pain.

Jennie wiped her hand across her face, in an unconscious gesture of revulsion at what she had done. Unconscious because as far as thought was concerned she was glad, glad that she had killed Satan.

"You . . . " Papa Anton gulped. "You. I did not think . . . that you too . . . . were plotting . . . . against my people."

"I . . . What do you mean?"

"The ancient . . . superstition of Satan's

. . . Night . . The fagots . . . driving them mad . . . with fear. I traced them to . . . "
His grey lips writhed. For a moment he could say no more.

What was he saying? Was he trying to tell her that someone else was Satan? But he was lying. He must be lying. Of course. He didn't know he was killed. He was trying to throw the blame on someone else. But before he died she must find out where the cages were. Maybe there were still some children there unchanged.

"Where is it?" Jennie asked. "The cellar with the cages? Where?"

"Cellar . . . " rasped from the man's throat. "Cages . . . I don't know . . . "

"Yes you do." Something, somewhere had been hammering at her mind, calling for her attention. Suddenly she knew what it was. One of the yellowed pictures on the wall, a picture of a pillared, low ceilinged chamber. A picture of the room where Satan had presided over his red altar.

She jabbed her finger at it. "You lie! What room is that? Where is that?"

He didn't look where she pointed, but he must have known what it was by the direction of her gesture, for words came again from his mouth, painfully.

"The crypt where we worshipped . . . before the church was finished. Behind it . . . . the vaults . . . . used to keep our honored dead secure against vandals . . . How do you know about it . . . ? Only stairs

outside here . . . . not used in years." Then a bubble of blood plopped from between his lips and his eyes closed.

THERE was no longer any sound in the little office, but there was a sound from outside, the sound of someone battering at the church's door. Someone had heard her shot, was trying to get in. Jennie thought that, then she forgot it. She was going through the office door, was in the great vault of the church proper, dark except for candles flickering before colored statues. There was one statue near by and the light of its candles fell on a space between two pillars right in front of her, and on a low, narrow door between them.

Jennie pulled at the iron handle of that door. It resisted her efforts. The pounding echoed and reechoed about her, and then the little door grated inward. She went through it.

It was pitch-dark in here, but she felt stone steps under her feet, going downwards. She went down them. They twisted spirally, twisted again, and light wavered against Jennie's eyes, a faint blue light outlining a narrow arch to which the steps twisted. She went through that arch and out into an open space.

The low-ceilinged, pillared space of the picture stretched before her. The blue light came from the other end, where the semi-circle of blue fires were low, the black fagots glowing embers. But there was enough light yet for her to see the red altar of Satan, a heap of gold and silver trinkets piled on it, the pitiful jewelry which the Sylvanians had brought with them from their homeland and treasured even when hungry mouths had gaped for the food that they would buy.

There was light enough to see the scarlet-cloaked, scarlet-hooded figure of Satan and to see him scooping the gold and silver from the altar and stuffing it within his cloak.

Jennie's hand lifted the gun, with infinite slowness. She had to be sure, very sure, that her first shot would bring him down. She might have no chance for another. She would certainly have no chance for another.

The gun was smashed out of her hand by a blow from the darkness beside her! A black form leaped out of the darkness, a calloused, filthy palm slapped across her face, cutting off her scream. There was the swirl of black draperies around her blinding her. Strong arms clamped around her body, pinioning her arms to her sides, lifting her from the ground.

"Got her, boss," a harsh voice husked. "Just in time."

"Good work," Satan's deep boom answered. "Good thing you heard her coming and hid there to meet her. Bring her here."

Jennie fought against the hold, twisted and squirmed. She was powerless against the terrible strength that held her, that carried her toward the place from which Satan's voice had come.

She gave up at last, just as she was laid down on some hard surface. The black stuff pulled away from her eyes and she saw the red form of Satan above her, knew that it was the demon's altar upon which she had been laid.

"I should have let her drown," the black monster grated. "Then she wouldn't a give us so much bother." Satan's red hand — red-gloved, Jennie saw, now that it was close to her — came out from within his cloak and something metallic gleamed in it. It stabbed her arm. "Too bad." Strangely he sounded sad, reluctant. "But now she will have to pay for that."

Pay. She was on the altar where Dickie had been before . . . before . . . . Jennie understood what he meant. What had happened to Dickie was going to happen to her!

The blue fire beat against the awesome

black form of her captor, against the more awesome scarlet apparition of his master. Satan's red hands lifted to his hood, pushed it back.

"You should not have interfered with me, Chennie," Mr. Erlauber's voice said. "You should have obeyed the warnings that I sent you twice." Satan's hands came away from his face *and it was Mr. Erlauber's face,* haggard, drawn. "Now you have made it dot I must do away with you."

Jennie stared up at the old German who she had thought her friend, the friend of all the downtrodden. Satan was — Otto Erlauber!

"I WAS growing old, Chennie, and my old bones could stand no longer the long hours and the hard work. So I struggled with temptation and lost, and I decided that my peculiar store of forbidden knowledge I should use to make comfortable my last few years. So the superstitions of the Sylvanians I played upon, hoping I should nod have to do more. But some of dem were stubborn, and I was greedy, and I went on and on, till now at the end I must destroy the one being I have ever loved."

"Don't weaken, boss," the man in black growled. "I'm in dis too, remember."

"No, I shall nod weaken. What I have begun I shall end, dough the end is so bitter. I do nod forget how loyal you have been, friend Joe."

"Damn right I've been loyal. Sneaking in the flats with my master key and dropping them sticks around, and picking the kids off the ladder after you got 'em fixed up with the stuff you put in the candy you give 'em. Come on. Let's get t'rough wid dis bimbo an' get out of here before sometin' else happens."

Mr. Erlauber! Joe! Much was explained, though more was unexplained, but to Jennie's agony of grief was added the agony of betrayal by the old man she

loved. Almost those agonies swamped her fear.

But that fear flared up in her full measure, searing through her brain, screaming in her chest, when she saw Erlauber's arm come up for the sweeping gesture she had once seen before, the circling sweep, learned from God alone knew what adept in magic somewhere in his long wanderings, that would change her into a mad dog. Death she would have welcomed, but to live on like that .... !

The gesture was never completed. A crash, a bawling voice stopped it. A voice that bawled out of the darkness, "Carlo. Geeve me back my Carlo," and a frenzied figure that came leaping out of the darkness, a wild-eyed, mad figure ahead of whom a pickaxe flailed to crash down into the skull of the black-cloaked hunchback, to lift again, dripping, arc through the air and sink into Otto Erlauber's chest.

Pavel Gorgio slipped in a gout of blood that spurted from Joe's shattered head, plunged into the red altar, crashed it over. Jennie slid off it, slid on top of the German's body, and she lay there unable to move, held by the paralysis with which his hypodermic had bound her.

Behind her she could hear Gorgio bawling, "Carlo! Where ees my Carlo?" And suddenly the trampling of many feet, the shouting of many voices.

"There he is," someone shouted. And someone else shouted, "Stop you, or I'll shoot!" But Pavel Gorgio, his wet undershirt clinging to the twisting muscles of his giant torso, lurched past her and plunged against the great rivet-studded door in the wall behind the altar. He was wrestling with a broad iron bar that lay in brackets across the door and held it closed. It came free, and the door swung inward.

It let through the sounds that Gorgio's frenzy-sharpened ears had heard through the barrier; the wail of children and a man's yell. The door was wide open and

Gorgio was grabbing a little boy in his arms, was hugging him to him.

But Jennie was looking past him. She saw other children clustering behind him. She saw a man, leaning wearily against the door jamb, covered with the slime and muck of sewer, but handsome to her as no Lothario of the screen could be . . . .

"*Bob*", his name ripped from her throat. "Oh Bob!"

"Jen!" her name husked from him. "Jen!" He shoved away from the door, shoved past Gorgio, was on his knees beside her. "Sweetheart!" His arms were around her . . .

And her arms were around him. The paralysis was gone. It had worn off quickly . . . .

"**C**RIPES!" someone exclaimed behind her, gruffly. "What's all this machinery?"

"Hell," another voice answered. "I'll be damned if that ain't a transformation table. I was stooge fer a stage magician before I got on the force and he had one just like it. He used to change women inter geese."

"Chees, that's no trick . . . . Holy mackerel! Look at them kids layin' there all tied up. I'll be . . . . "

Jennie was on her feet. Two cops were shining their flashlights at the other side of the altar table Gorgio had thrown over. She ran around its end, not daring yet to hope . . . .

Springs, gleaming steel wires, were a jumble behind the dais' top. And, on the stone floor the platform had covered, two children lay, bound and gagged, red-haired little Marta and — Dickie! Dickie, tied up, bedraggled but in his own shape, and alive!

Jennie was dimly aware of the cop's voice going on. "He'd put the goose on that kinda shelf there an he'd lay the gal up on top of the table. Then he'd t'row some magnesium powder in a fire in front of the table. When it blazed so the aujience cudn't see, he'd kick that there pedal and zingo, the gal' ud drop down an' the goose ud pop up where she had been."

Jennie heard that and recalled it afterwards, but just now she was aware only that she hugged her little brother to her breast.

MATTERS had quieted down a little later. Jennie had told her story to the cops, they believed it now, and it was Bob's turn.

"I saw Jennie here for a minute on my way to work, and was a bit worried about the way she looked, but she rushed me off to my job and it didn't sink in properly. After a while I realized that something must be dreadfully wrong, and I took a chance on locking up and running up to her flat to find out what was up. The door was unlocked, but the flat was empty.

"I was scared stiff by then. I knocked at the Gorgio's, next door and after awhile the woman opened a slit. All I could make out from her was something about the firescape, but that was enough. I had wondered why the firescape window was open, because Jennie always kept it locked. I went down the ladder and found a hole in the backyard. A piece of Jennie's dress was torn off on the edge of the rusted manhole rim.

"I went down into it, found an abandoned sewer. What Jennie and Dick could be up to in there was more than I could understand, but I took out after them. I don't know how far I had gone before I heard sounds like the barking of doors, made out a ladder and climbed up to a ledge.

"The sounds were coming from the other side of what was apparently a blank wall. I fumbled at it, caught my hand in a metal ring, pulled on it. The wall started to open.

"What I saw you've already heard. The

hunchback knocked me into the pool, I guess it was once a trap to hold backwater from an unusually high tide. He crouched on the edge, watching for me to come up. I knew if I did he'd finish me, and I also knew that the longer he watched for me the better chance Jennie had to get away, so I stayed down under the surface as long as I could, and then just let my nose pop out.

"It wasn't long before Joe got tired and chinned himself back up out of the sewer. He closed the door in the wall, but that was easy to open, and I got out into that room with the cages .... I couldn't get the door open but I could pick the padlocks with my pocket knife and get the kids out of there. Then I heard faint sounds of all Hell breaking loose other side the door, and Carlo Gorgio ran to it, yelling, Papa! That's all, I guess."

There was a call from the stairs at the end of the crypt. "Hey sergeant! Is it all right for the ambulance to take the father away?"

"Sure. We can get his statement in the hospital."

"His statement?" Jennie cried out. "Is it Papa Anton you mean? Is he alive?"

"Sure, miss. Your bullet just ripped his side and knocked him out, but he'll be all right after a week or two in the hospital."

"Oh thank God," Jennie breathed. "Thank God."

* * *

Much later, when Dickie was asleep in his bed and Bob and she, cleaned up, were talking it all over again in the living room, Jennie thought of something. "You know," she said. "I wonder if Mr. Erlauber really meant to do anything to me. Maybe Joe didn't know the changes were just hocus pocus. Maybe Mr. Erlauber just meant to drop into the bottom part of the table, and gave me the injection so I wouldn't cry out and Joe would think he really had made me disappear?"

"Perhaps," Bob said slowly. "A man who has been the soul of goodness all his life cannot turn wholly evil over night. After all, if it had not been for the mad dog's escaping and your shooting Papa Anton, no one would have been physically hurt by his scheme, although those poor Sylvanians did mentally suffer the tortures of the damned. The children would eventually have been found in the cages, or under the magician's table."

"That's right. Oh Bob, it isn't wicked to be a little sorry for him, is it? He — he said I was the only one he ever loved."

"But he's not the only one who ever loved you, Jen. If that's wisdom, then I'm the wisest man who ever lived."

"Bob!"

Bob Coffey was destined to win many honors in his chosen profession, but never one he prized as greatly as the accolade of soft lips he received then.

THE END

DEATH UNMASKS
AT MIDNIGHT

By NAT SCHACHNER

(Author of "The Kiss of the Iron Maiden," etc.)

Surging out of the grim, gaunt houses of the murky mining town came the green bloated creatures that once were human—to clutch with loathsome fingers at Steve Bedford as he stumbled to save his sweetheart from the mad masquerade where death lead the dancers while pestilence piped the tune.

A WAN glimmer of light pierced the darkling sky. The moon floated invisibly above the floor of clouds, irradiated a vague greyness over Cross Bones Gulch. Objects pricked into view and disclosed themselves to Steve Bedford's straining eyes as he stumbled along the twisting mountain road.

Fear drove Steve's feet to frantic haste —not fear for himself but for lovely Gail Wentworth, who only five days before had promised to be his wife. Hardly had he begun to guess at the happiness that would be his when there had come a cryptic telegram from Gail's guardian summoning her enigmatically to the

An Eerily Gripping Novelette of the Black, Irresistible Menace that Brought Death and Madness in its Wake.

colony of wealthy wastrels and second generation spenders that was situated at the upper end of the mining town in Cross Bones Gulch.

There the dissolute sons and daughters of the men who had discovered the Cross Bones mines lived in luxury and spent the gold that came from Gulch in the feverish pursuit of pleasure. There they whipped their jaded appetites with mad parties and morbid panderings to perverted tastes. There Gail had been for four days—and had not answered his wires.

Anxiety had become agony, until Steve thought he could stand it no longer. With the arrival of the fifth day he had started out to drive the four hundred miles to the Gulch, only to find when he was almost at his goal that the road was barred by a giant log on which was lettered the dire inscription: FLEE THE WRATH OF THE LORD! THE CURSE OF HELL IS ON THIS TOWN!

There was nothing to do but finish the last few miles on foot. Steve stumbled on.

The mining town loomed directly ahead. Tall, gaunt smokestacks, limned indelibly against a backwash of hills; huge, formless buildings, obviously smelters, eyeless and blank. Great scars in the mountainside grey with unholy pallor; monstrous, clutching fingers that must be derricks; a tumble of blurred, elongated shapes that should be sluices.

And suddenly, his hurrying feet were echoing loudly between ramshackle, crazily leaning houses. He was in the town, in the squalid meanness where the miners passed their futile, grimy lives, coming from long shifts to homes with slattern wives and sprawling litters of children.

But the houses mocked him as he passed. They were dead, dead as the mines beyond, dead as the street down whose filth-laden length he moved. Unconsciously he had flicked off his light, yielding to a strange inner impulse. His nose wrinkled, snuffed the moveless air. A smell as of a charnel house breathed over him, fetid, corrupt, foul with unmistakable odors. In God's name what was wrong with Cross Bones Gulch?

Suddenly he knew. With a strangled cry he caromed off the bloated thing that lay sodden and inert in his path. His finger flicked tremblingly at the torch's trigger. He *must* see what it was into which his foot had sunk with a horrible, squishing sound. The brilliant pencil stabbed at the thing that lay almost at his feet, brought out each detail into dreadful clarity.

Once it had been a man! Now it was a shapeless, ballooning mass. The grey skin was tight to bursting over the flesh beneath, and the lolling head was puffed to far beyond its normal limits. But what made Steve stagger back in violent retching was the color of that head. The half-clad body was clammy grey, the swollen arm that clutched with scraping fingers at the earth was gray, but that which seemed a face was *green*, a mottled green such as forms on stagnant pools.

Steve's stumbling, backward thrust brought him crunching into hideous softness behind. A scream aborted in the taut muscles of his throat as he threw himself desperately forward. Without looking he knew what it was. Another bloated corpse. The light had flicked out in his first agony of repulsion. Now he dared not turn it on again. He stood there, crouched, panting, trying to control his shuddering nerves.

The street was a litter of corpses, swollen bodies with putrescent green faces. The sheer horror of it smote him like a blow. He was alone in a city of the nameless dead! Some dreadful Thing had passed with pestilential wings over the Gulch and left it a charnel house, a plague-stricken emptiness.

An irresistible impulse to turn and flee up the road he had come boiled in Steve's veins. He had already swung around, blindly, fearfully. Then Gail's face rose in anguished vision to torment him. Her arms were extended, imploring. A white skeleton arm extended from the background of his imagination to seize the girl and pull her shrieking into the enfolding darkness.

The imagined cries still rang in his ears as Steve flung himself down the corpse-strewn street. Gail Wentworth had told him what the Gulch was like. The long single street extended down its meandering length. First came the squalid huts of the miners, then mine pits and the smelters; then, as the Gulch widened into a park-like slope, the first of the great houses of the owners. A different community, a different world. Its inhabitants looked down with cynical indifference upon the filth and clamor of the wretched hole from which their luxuriance flowed. They were a race apart, gay, heedless, stifling their boredom with ceaseless pleasures, dancing with precarious feet on the ragged edge of disaster.

UP there was Gail Wentworth. Her father had, during his life, wisely sent her to school and normal surroundings in the outside world. Up there, first of the mansions, was the home of Rufus Trumbull, her guardian, who had signed the cryptic telegram that had brought her back in such haste.

Steve gritted his teeth and lurched ahead, threading his way up the stench-filled street, trying desparately to avoid the balloon-like bodies. The pounding in his ears grew louder. A rustle of movement ran like a slender strand through the thumping of his heart. It insinuated itself subtly into the greater noise. Imagination, panic, he whispered to himself, while his senses clamored the truth. Stealthy feet were padding after him, slithering along crumbling earth, scrambling over corruption-bloated bodies. With an oath at his own jangled nerves Steve whirled suddenly around.

The grey, filtering light made the street behind him more hideous than ever. The two-story houses that lined its twisting path were gaunt, scabby skeletons of ruinous disrepair. But they were no longer dead! Dim-seen figures erupted from yawning doorways, flowed in silent tottering procession behind him.

Creatures that might once have been alive, but now were ghosts of the departed town, furious at this rash intruder into their festering silence. Men there were, dressed in overalls like miners, tall and lank, with coal-black eyes burning from smudged countenances. Women too, features pinched and wan, hair awry, skinny arms upraised from ragged shawls in voiceless exhortation.

The stealthy procession stopped as Steve whirled around. For a long moment they stared at each other in deathly silence. A glacial wind stirred over Steve's body, froze the very blood in his veins. What did it all mean? Who were these ghouls of the night who crept after him on tottering legs? What were those green-faced corpses that littered the street? Into what abode of the damned had he unwittingly intruded?

The withheld breath exploded through his lips in a shuddering gasp. An answering quaver rippled over the figures that hunched behind. The quaver rose to a mutter, the mutter of a wild, screeching cacophony of sound. Lank figures writhed in inarticulate fury, hate blazed in sunken sockets, and fists knotted and gesticulated in the semi-gloom.

Suddenly the ranks swayed and split as if cloven by a shouldering prow. A thing staggered forth, shrieking and sobbing. Steve stared at it in blasting horror.

The thing was a caricature of a man. Its body was gross and bloated beyond all imagining. Its face was puffed and green. Toneless shrieks poured from lips that seemed stretched to bursting. Then suddenly, as the others tumbled hastily away, it spun around, gyrated in hideous dance, and flopped headlong to the earth. There it lay, moveless, sprawled, a puffed-out, shapeless corpse, even as the others.

The grey creatures swung around and past the body. They surged up the street, filling it from wall to wall. A low, deadly snarl, more horrible than any cry, exhaled from their lips. Their faces were masks of utter hate. Knotted arms clawed forth, eager to reach and rend him.

STEVE awoke from his stupor. They were coming for him, these things from hell! He turned swiftly and raced up the winding road. Behind him the snarl became a high-pitched clamor, the howling of animals lusting for the kill.

The houses gave way to mine pits, the gashed mountainside to the smelters. The thudding of many feet swept after him. They were gaining. A note of triumph hounded in their cries.

Steve glanced desperately from side to side even as he ran. Nowhere was there shelter from the ravening pursuit. The mountain walls narrowed and hemmed him in. The buildings were vacant and tenantless. Up beyond, he knew, stretched the community of the owners. But it was a pocket, a wider slope in the Gulch, surrounded by unscalable cliffs. There was no other egress but the way by which he had entered.

And suppose—the thought almost paralyzed his pounding legs—they too were dead, or transformed into screeching things of the night. Gail! The name swelled in his throat, poured forth in a cry as fierce as those that echoed behind him. It could not be! She *must* be there, still alive, still safe. He must get to her before these nightmare monstrosities did; he must shield her from their screaming hate.

SUDDENLY he was racing over a bridge, a wooden structure that spanned a dark-flowing flood beneath. It was the mountain torrent that separated the homes of the owners from the mining town and fed the sluices down below. A grey wall rose before him, high, surmounted with barbed wire and broken glass. A gate, closed, unscalable, barred his path. He flung his weary legs toward it, his lead-heavy arm raised to batter at the portal.

Already the vanguard of the hideous mob was clattering over the bridge, screeching with vengeful fury. Before he could raise the occupants within—if any there were—before they could unfasten the heavy bars, the clamoring things would be upon him, rending him. . . .

Figures flowed out of the night, surrounded him. Gun muzzles gleamed evilly in the dimness.

"Get back where you came from," a voice snarled, "afore I plug you!"

Steve dropped his battering fist from the solid wood. There were three of them, hard-faced, tough-looking men. Holsters dangled from their sides, and guns pointed directly at him. But there was open, jittery terror in their eyes, and they wetted their lips with nervous tongues. Nor did they come near him. They kept five paces away.

"For God's sake," Steve cried, "let me in! Can't you see they're after me?"

"Can't let no one in," growled the man who had first spoken. But there was a quaver of dread in his voice as his eyes flicked back to the bridge. The wooden planks resounded with the clatter of the ghouls. They were only fifty yards distant.

"Get back, you devils," the guard shouted suddenly. "I'll shoot."

A weird, mouthing cry rose from the rushing mob. Their panting hate grew louder as they came on and on. The man raised his weapon. It spat flame, stabbed the night with its racket.

A figure stumbled, went down. The others trampled over him as they surged forward. Guns roared again and again. Figures gesticulated, crashed headlong. But the horde rolled on, a tide of screeching demons.

"Jeez!" groaned a guard. "If they touch us, we're goners."

"The gate, you fools!" Steve shouted. "Open the gate!"

The leader backed away from him in cowering fear as he sprang forward.

"Don't you come near me," he quavered, "or I'll shoot yuh down."

A figure separated itself from the grey tide, a tall thing clad in miner's denim. It flung itself upon the back of the unsuspecting man in a great leap. The guard screamed as bony fingers clawed for his throat. His gun jerked. Flame spurted directly at his assailant. The figure screeched, and both went tumbling and thrashing to the ground.

The thudding torrent was not twenty feet away. Steve could see the insane blaze of their eyes, the frenzied contortions of their faces. Hinges creaked behind him. Steve whirled. The two surviving guards were swinging the gate wide with frantic haste. He raced forward, brushed against them as all three clattered through the opening.

The men swerved with cries of fear. The guns dropped from paralyzed fingers; they jerked away from him as if he were the Devil himself. In another second they were racing in wild flight through the enveloping darkness.

Steve had no time to wonder at the strangeness of their actions. The horde was almost upon him. His shoulder rammed with desperate strength against the massive timbers. Slowly, very slowly, the gate creaked back into place. Frantically his fingers jerked at the huge iron bar, slammed it into its socket just as the weird creatures smashed headlong into the barrier.

Wild screams, furious mouthings penetrated the foot-thick logs. But Steve leaned weakly against its comforting hardness. All the strength seemed suddenly to have quit his panting frame. The gate staggered under terrific blows, shook with vibration. Wearily he straightened up. He must find Gail!

"Stand where you are and let me look you over!" a voice warned, icily calm.

CHAPTER TWO

Home of Dark Disaster

STEVE jerked around, stopped short, arms straining at his sides. A figure moved forward from the black shelter of an elm, came to a halt a few yards away.

"They're afraid to come closer to me," Steve thought dully. Then he sucked in breath with a whistling sound.

The man was tall, almost as tall as himself. A gun pointed with steady aim at Steve. Bitter black eyes gleamed in a dark, saturnine face. A close-cropped, grey mustache surmounted thin, tight-pressed lips. But it was the man's costume that engrossed Steve's gaze. It was a single, molded sheath of silken stuff, enclosing him from neck to foot. Its color was green; mottled, streaked. Horror prickled slowly at Steve's scalp. The green seemed the slimy green of those corpses in the village street below. And on his silken breast a death's head grinned with white, fleshless laughter.

The gun moved threateningly.

"Speak up! Who are you?"

Obviously, the man in green was accustomed to be obeyed. He seemed to pay no heed to the animal-like cries of the mob outside his gate as he watched Steve with wary eyes.

The young man gulped. It was hard for him to tear his gaze away from that weird costume. His voice steadied.

"I am Stephen Bedford," he answered evenly. "I came here to find my fiancee, Gail Wentworth, and her trustee, Rufus Trumbull. Down in Cross Bones Gulch I found death and corruption." He shivered. "The houses poured out creatures who wanted to tear me to pieces. Naturally I ran. Listen to them."

But the green-clad man paid no attention to the pounding and screaming. His eyes hardened on Steve. His gun was rigid.

"So you're Steve Bedford," he repeated. "And you want Gail and Rufus Trumbull."

Suddenly his head went back and harsh laughter welled from his throat. It ripped through the night, overtopped and beat down the clamor without. As if they had heard their master, the things outside ceased their cries. Slow snufflings as of animals in abject terror sounded over the walls. Then feet shuffled, dragged stealthily over scraping gravel. Soon there was silence, sinister, ominous.

A great fear swept over Steve. His fists clenched. His eyes went sideways to the dull gleam of the automatic that had fallen to the grass from hands of the frightened guard.

"You know them then?" he asked. "Who are you and what have you done with Gail?"

Imperceptibly his feet slid along the smooth carpet of grass. If only he could get to that gun, sweep it up in one quick movement—

"I," said the man with strange intonation, "am Rufus Trumbull."

Steve staggered as if he had been struck. "You!" he cried hoarsely. "You Rufus Trumbull!" This man, clad in mottled green, was the trustee who controlled Gail's money, the man whose urgent telegram had brought Gail to this valley of fear and horror—for what dreadful purpose, to what hideous doom?

Anger burned in his veins. He forgot the gun, he forgot everything but the thought of the girl he loved. He went forward, teeth bared, shoulders hunched.

"What have you done with her?" he demanded hoarsely. "If you've hurt her—"

The man shrank away from his slow advance. Terror leaped into his eyes.

"Stay back, Bedford," he shouted. "I'll shoot! Gail's all right—yet."

Steve rocked back on his heels. "What do you mean—yet?"

The fear ebbed from Trumbull. He laughed, and there was bitter cynicism in his laugh.

"I mean just that, young man," he chuckled. He slipped the gun into a pocket in his silken costume. It made a sinister bulge of green. "She was alive a minute ago. She may be dead now. It does not matter much."

"Dead!" Steve echoed foolishly. His brain whirled on an axis of baffled horror. What did it all mean, this mocking japery, this strange-costumed man who stood before him and spoke of his beloved's death so callously? "By God, Trumbull!" he swore, raising his fist. "If—"

"Fool!" the man spat at him contemptuously. "We are all dead. You and I and Gail and every one in that house of mine. What does it matter when we die? Now or in half an hour or at midnight. By tomorrow's sun we shall all be dead. Dead, do you hear?" he screamed hysterically. "We are doomed, doomed!"

He whirled quickly and went slamming up the gravel path into enswathing blackness, crying all the while:

"Doomed! Doomed!"

STEVE stepped mechanically after him. Triphammers pounded in his skull, shattering his thoughts. It was better so. He dared not think; only action, swift and muscular, would save him from gibbering madness.

Trumbull's fleeing feet raced far ahead, and Steve followed, holding to the crunching gravel as the path wound through dark enclosing oaks. Then, suddenly, he was in the open; a vast, dim expanse of upland lawn. Directly ahead lights blazed, pricking out with yellow flares the oblong windows of a great house. Trumbull's house! Gail had told him about it; of its huge size and myriad rooms of curious shapes and colors.

Trumbull had disappeared. The night was still, the house for all its lights a tomb of silences. Nothing stirred. Nothing moved. Even the howling creatures that had spewed from Cross Bones Gulch seemed to have retreated into their secret lairs.

Steve did not hesitate. Hard-eyed, dry of mouth and throat, he started for the house. Trumbull had said Gail was alive. She must be there. Hideous danger threatened her. He must get to her at once. His knuckles on the carven oak clamored interminably. There was no answer, no responding stir. The yellow light from casement windows too high for spying glances streamed out over the lawn in a mockery of welcome. Shadows crossed and recrossed in ghostly movement. Steve, half turned, saw the fantastic shadows. His mouth was grim and his heart a suffocating burden. He knocked again, furiously. Blood trickled from his knuckles.

"Open!" he shouted.

The shadows on the lawn froze. Their ghostly counterparts within had stopped their ceaseless movements, as if they were listening to this rash intruder.

"Open, or I'll break in!" he cried again, and put his shoulder to the solid oak.

Noiselessly, on well-oiled hinges, the portal yielded. Steve straightened, panting slightly, wary for unseen menace. He cursed himself for not having picked up the guard's discarded gun.

A figure in black stood in the shadows of the unlit entry. A florid, frightened face peered out at him, and jerked back with a little quavering cry.

"Who—who are you? You're not one of the guests, sir." A butler, funereal in costume, correct in manner, but trembling as with the ague.

"You're damned right I'm not!" Steve growled. "I want to see Miss Wentworth, and right away! Do you hear?"

The butler swung suddenly on the door. Steve had not thought he could move so fast. With a muttered oath Steve crashed into the closing door, hurled it violently open. The black-clad man screeched, and fled into the tunnel-like opening to the left as if all the devils in hell were at his back.

Steve disregarded him, strode on clicking heels across the smooth parquet flooring toward the rear. Sombre curtains obscured what lay beyond. He flung them open, and stood a moment, blinking in the weird illumination, aghast at what he saw.

It was a great ballroom, festooned in drapes that hung sheer from ceiling to floor. High overhead, suspended from an arched ceiling, was a huge crystal chandelier of a thousand iridescent pieces. Slowly, very slowly it revolved, and, as it turned, light from some invisible source within flooded the huge room with eerie radiance.

A minute before it had been yellow,

yellow as brimstone spewed from Vesuvius; now it was green, green with the scum that grows on drowned men, green as the corpse-faces that lay in Cross Bones Gulch, green as the trappings that Trumbull had worn. The color deepened and cast its scabrous shade over a great figure seated in ghastly solitude on a dais at the farther end of the room.

Steve stood fixed in terror as he stared unbelievingly at its awful form. It bore the semblance of a corpse, with bloated belly and shapeless, grinning head. Its body was the grey of weltering clouds and stormy seas; its head a mottled green. It *must* be paper—plaster—a composition of some sort—Steve told himself desperately. But its eyes stared upon the stricken watcher as if life crawled within its immobile frame.

With a tremendous effort Steve swung his gaze from the seated death to the fantastic figures on the floor. Even as he did, music filled the room with soft clamor and curious chords, like the humming in the head of a man dying of fever. As if they were marionettes on a string, the masked apparitions jerked into a dance, swinging in close couples over the polished floor, pirouetting in dervish like whirls, weaving in and out in grotesque glissades.

Steve's skin ridged into little mounds over gelid flesh. Had he gone mad or was he actually seeing these things? The light had shifted to a scarlet, beaded froth. It drenched the maskers in a bath of blood.

Horned and hooded devils capered with mermaids with rigid white faces and scaly bodies. A shaggy Pan stamped his cloven hoofs before admiring witches carrying brooms. Green-silked beings, like Trumbull, with dragon heads, swung and dipped to the lascivious swaying of sirens whose hair was falsely yellow and whose faces were painted wax.

They did not seem to see Steve, or seeing, paid no heed. On and on they danced, while the light shifted through strange chords of color, to the darkened prismatic tonalities of an invisible orchestra. "The Island of the Dead" it was, the macabre imaginings of Rachmaninoff, played with devilish skill, and plucking to snapped chords as the evocated corpses sank shuddering back upon their biers.

The music stopped. The dancers lay inert as if the strings that jerked them had fallen from lifeless hands. Mutterings arose, the rustling murmurs of unintelligible conversation. Laughter swelled, shrill, strained, edged with hysteria.

It was that laughter which broke the spell that bound the watcher. He strode grimly into the room, though every cell in his benumbed brain shrieked warning to flee from this hall of fantastic horrors. The masked dancers froze, turned sinister, covered faces to the unbidden guest.

A GIRL'S shriek rose jagged and sharp over the sudden silence. It sliced through Steve's flesh like a thirsty knife, it sent the blood roaring through his temples. He'd recognized that voice among a million counter sounds.

"Gail!" he shouted, "where are you? I'm coming!" Already he was lunging down the length of the hall in the direction from which that cry of fear had seemed to come.

The masked monstrosities shrank from his headlong course in sundering waves, then closed behind him in a surge of movement that cut off all egress. But Steve's whole clamoring being was concentrated on that frightened scream of the girl he loved. Where was she? What had been done to her?

He saw her then, backed against the dun drapes of the farther wall. Her eyes were wide on something that lay huddled almost at her feet. Her stiffened fingers still held the silken mask she had torn from her face. She wore a queen's robe, bright red and trailing, while on her lovely golden hair a tinsel crown hung crazily askew.

"Steve!" With a moan of fear she flung out her arms at the sight of him, stumbled in panting haste from the grisly thing before her. "Steve darling! Take me away from this dreadful place! Take me away!"

A green-encased man with dragon's head and fleshless skull white on his breast whipped after her, caught her in a grip of steel.

"You fool!" The hollow, distorted voice echoed queerly with the mask. "This man has just come in from the outside, and death has entered with him. Don't touch him; don't even go near him. And put on your mask. Remember the pledge."

"I never took your pledge," Gail cried hysterically, wrenching vainly at his hold. "Let me go! I'm afraid of this ghastly mummery. Death is among us. We mocked him and he came unbidden. Steve, Steve!"

The young man made the intervening distance in a rush. His arm shot out, sent the green-clad figure sprawling violently away from the girl.

"Damn you!" he shouted. "You're at the bottom of this hellish business, Trumbull, and I think I know why. If you try to . . ."

He broke off in amazement. Five other green-clad figures, identical in every detail, had ranged themselves by the side of the man he had flung away. Green dragon faces, hideous, leering, snouted at him from six identic heads.

Steve's grip tightened on the clinging body of the girl. "Steve darling," she whispered desperately. "Let's get out of this dreadful place. It's been a nightmare ever since—"

"It's too late!" A sepulchral voice sounded from one of the grinning masks. Steve could not tell from which it issued.

"Death has entered even while we mocked. The breath of corruption is among us. We are doomed. One by one and each by each! Look!"

A moan went up from the crowding fantastics, a gasp compounded of horror and deadly fear. Steve, with Gail cold and shivering in the crook of his arm, felt the fingers of death drum along his spine.

For the thing that had fallen almost at Gail's feet was a ballooning corpse, swelling its green-silk covering until it split in a hundred different places and showed the bursting, greyish flesh beneath. The knowledge seared through Steve that underneath that vermilion dragon's mask the face was a green, shapeless putty. Whatever it was that had littered the street of Cross Bones Gulch with its hideous handiwork had invaded the haughty walls of Trumbull's pleasure house.

A woman screamed, short, sharp, sudden, like the yelping of a dog in pain. A mermaid, trailing a long scaly tail behind her ample form, staggered out of the fear-stricken mass, jerked toward the huddled body. She stopped suddenly, five paces away, her feet skidding with desperate effort to stop herself. Her white, set face was a staring, unwinking mask.

"It's Rufus!" she screeched. "I know it is. Some one take that mask off. My poor husband!"

A mirthless chuckle broke from one of the green-clad men.

"Take it off yourself, Lora, if you are Lora Trumbull. Who has a better right than you?"

The white-masked mermaid shrank away with a shiver that swished her scaly tail over the floor.

"No, no," she whispered. "It's the plague. It kills by a touch. I'd get it!"

She backed away in feverish haste, the terror seeping through her unmoving mask. Some one laughed. A nasty, mocking laugh. As if it were a signal, a wind of merriment swept the crowding masks. It grew wild, hysterical, sinister. It waxed to a gale of mouthing sounds, of ghastly jeering. The great room of dreadful maskers swayed and writhed with side splitting mirth. The mirth of the damned, the frozen laughter of those about to die. They gripped each other and danced with wild abandon. Spasmodic, jerking cries rose from them.

"Lora's afraid!"

"Afraid it might *not* be Rufus!"

"Where's Oliver Brearley? He'll comfort her. He always does!"

"Irene Brearley's her best friend, too."

"That's what best friends are for."

"Maybe it's Oliver lying there."

"I'm *so* thrilled, my dear, aren't you?"

"It was a swell idea in the beginning. It's better now."

"We can't unmask until the stroke of midnight. I'm dying to know who's dead."

"What does it matter? The plague has breathed upon us. We'll all be swollen corruption by then."

"Not I. I expect to be the only one alive. It means millions."

"Whose idea was it? That whoever survives at midnight should be the beneficiaries of our joint estates?"

"I think Fisher Duane's. Rufus was the one who suggested this ball as a sort of defiance to the Plague and all its works. They're dying by the hundreds in the mining town. And we can't get out."

"Got his idea from Poe's *Masque of the Red Death.*"

"*Brrr!* Remember what happened there. How Death was one of the maskers, and at midnight revealed himself?"

"*Sssh!* You give me the creeps. Suppose Death heard our challenge and took it up."

"Righto! Maybe I'm Death, ha, ha! You can't tell who I am, and I won't know you either until midnight."

The revelers fell away from the speaker. Laughter dropped from them. Scared whisperings took its place. Perhaps, who could tell? A cold wind swept them all, broke them away from each other, distrustful, shivering. Death was among them, unseen, stalking their ranks, putting his bony finger upon them.

Soon the scoffers would fall, writhing and screaming, while *he*— The red-clad devil with painted horns and scarlet hood who had distilled the poison of fear into them chuckled hollowly, alone, an eddy in the swirling mass that edged farther and farther away from him.

CHAPTER THREE

Plague's Mad Mistress

LORA TRUMBULL heard the laughter, felt the jeering cruelty of those shouted words. All her secrets were being ruthlessly exposed to mockery by those she had thought friends, now masked and hateful in anonymous slander.

If Rufus were not that loathsome corpse, then his vengeance would be swift and deadly. She knew his burning jealousy; she had encountered and braved it out at times when he had nothing to feed it on. But now—

She turned and ran blindly, awkwardly, down the long hall. Her green fish tail trailed behind her in swishing travesty.

"Damn you! Damn you all!" she mouthed through her white plaster mask. "A bunch of rotten, evil wasters, dancing on the edge of eternity. You have sneered at God and mocked at the devil. You shut yourselves up in this place while the poor people lifted plague-stricken hands from the village and begged for help. You're nasty, crawling vermin, all of you. The plague has come; you can't escape it any more. By midnight death will touch you, one by one, and I—I alone shall live, heir to all the syndicate, owner of Cross Bones and all its riches."

She was screaming and laughing wildly as she ran past the suddenly hushed throng of maskers and through a green-draped door into the chamber beyond. As the somber drape fell back into place the shrill cackle of her voice broke off into abrupt silence.

They looked at each other then, tight masks sheltering the suspicion, the deadly fear that lurked beneath. Yet no one stirred. Was Rufus Trumbull alive, or was he that thing which lay sodden on the floor? If he were alive, he made no move to follow his wife, no sign to disclose his presence.

Steve's scalp was a prickling horror. Gail clung to him, her lovely features drained white. They were the only two without masks.

"STEVE!" she implored. "We must get out. They are not human any more, not one of them. That telegram I received was a blind to get me here. Rufus claims he never sent it. The plague was raging in the town and I couldn't go back. No one would take me. They wanted me to join their terrible scheme, to sign the joint will leaving everything to the survivors. I refused. Rufus laughed and said it didn't matter. I was a minor, and he as trustee could sign for me. He did. I'm afraid of him; I think the whole thing's his plot to gain control of Cross Bones Gulch. They discovered last week a new vein of gold. It's worth millions."

Steve pressed her tight. His jaw was rigid.

"We're going, Gail, even if I have to fight my way through."

He swung around, took a quick step toward the massed throng between him and the entrance.

"Stop!" A green-swathed man with dragon head was at his side. "You can't escape. You came unbidden and you must remain." The others clad like him had scattered, were merged among the nightmare figures that dotted the room.

Steve pushed Gail behind him and confronted the apparition with knotted fists. His voice was low and hard.

"Just try and stop me."

The man chuckled mirthlessly.

"I don't have to. It's been done. This is a sporting proposition. We didn't want any one to welch. We're all in the same boat. So we wired the doors and windows. The juice is running through them now. It's death to leave."

"I don't scare easily," snarled Steve. "Come on, Gail."

"Look!" The chilling, muffled voice resumed. "There's someone who has broken. It'll be a good example for the others."

A green figure was running furiously for the heavily draped entrance.

"I can't stand it any more," he screeched. "We're caught here like rats. I'd rather—"

His gloved hand reached out, clawed at the black velvet stuffs. A blinding flash shot through the hall. Flame crackled and leaped from the curtains to the doomed man, wrapped him around in a halo of hellish light. He jerked in a devil's dance, gyrated, and crashed headlong with a shriek of utter agony. Then he lay very still, while the stench of sizzling flesh seeped through the hall.

GAIL caught hold of Steve to keep from falling. A horrified moan burst through her tight-locked lips. Steve felt sick. But the dragon-headed man nearby exclaimed in satisfaction:

"The fool! He knew we had the hangings and all our costumes saturated in a saline solution to make them good conductors. He must have gone mad. Well,

it means more money for those who are left."

Steve turned convulsively. An overwhelming desire seized him to smash that nightmare dragon head, to see what manner of man lay beneath, to still that callous tongue. Then he stared. The man had disappeared, was lost in the heaving, exclaiming mob of maskers.

Gail looked up at him with quiet despair. Her face was white but brave.

"That poor fellow was right. We're trapped like rats. There's a fiend among us who instilled the poison of his suggestions into these men and women. They welcomed it as a grand gesture to the plague, as a fitting climax to empty, worthless lives. He moved them like puppets on a string. And now he has them caught. No matter how they struggle, they'll die. And I'm marked too. My share in the syndicate is too big to let slip."

Steve's grip tightened on her. "Never, darling. I'll find Rufus Trumbull and choke the vicious life out of him first."

"You won't find him. There are six of the bigger shareholders dressed all like. You can't tell them apart. Besides, it might not be he. The ball was his idea, but the will was Fisher Duane's. And Brearley hated him because of Lora. He was crazy about her, and Irene, his wife, knew it, though Rufus didn't."

The hall was a pandemonium. Devils and mermaids and Pans and witches ran, screaming frantically, in all directions. Panic had seized them, blind and terrible. Yet even as they ebbed and flowed, like a fatal tide they shrank away from the door where the still-smoking body lay, from the spot where the plague-stricken corpse was already corruption. And, towering over the devil's throng in leering awfulness, was the seated representation of death, the insanely clever fashioning of some perverted brain.

Steve shouted suddenly. His voice

flamed through the confusion, brought a hush to the frightened masqueraders.

"Listen, all of you," he bellowed. "You've been fooled; you've been brought here to die. The plague was the pretext. It's your money the hidden fiend is after. He's one of the green men. Strip them, unmask them, see who they are, and put an end to their frightful terror. It's the only way you can save yourselves."

The fantastic revelers stopped short as the idea entered their muddled minds. Then a murmur went over them, and grew. Soon it would be a full-throated snarl of rage. This unknown, unmasked man was right. They had been tricked. In another second. Already Steve had turned exultantly, seeking the first he could lunge for with crushing fists.

"Stand where you are."

Clear and cold and accustomed to command rose the voice. Three green-silked men with snarling, vermilion dragon masks stood in a compact knot close to the seated simulacrum of death, almost touching its grisly belly. Automatics were dull lights in their gloved hands and they swept the throng with deadly aim. The center one snouted directly at Steve. The young man held his ground, making no further move, watching his chance with alert mind and searching eye. Gail stood proudly by his side, steady and unafraid.

"You *are* fools," the hidden voice crackled. It was most impossible to tell from which mask it issued. "The plague is no pretext. It came five days ago below, no one knows from where. It spread like wildfire. Men screamed and died on the instant. We were cut off from escape. The only way out of the Gulch is through the pest-ridden village. Our only chance was to close ourselves up, away from the plague. We prided ourselves on our cynicism, our sporting instincts. If we must die, let us die like men and women who fear nothing, not even death. That was the

idea of this masquerade. It's our defiance to any gods there are; the thumbing of our noses at fate. It's been a wonderful gesture. Let's not spoil it now by whining."

"But the plague is here. We'll all be dead by morning," some one cried from the cowering mob.

The masked voice was edged with contempt. "You'll be just as dead if you run like cowards into the village. The germs are in us already; we'll have to take our chances. Those who survive will own all Cross Bones Gulch; those who don't—nothing will matter to them."

"It's a lie," Steve said harshly. "One of you knows exactly what it's all about. One of you has engineered this in cold blood. One of you will remain alive while your dupes die in horrible fashion."

"Damn you!" the hidden voice called hoarsely. "I ought to kill you for that. You're trying to breed suspicion among us."

Which was just what Steve had intended. And even as he poised on the balls of his feet, ready to fling himself sideways at the first tightening of fingers on triggers, he noted that his stratagem had worked. Stealthily, seemingly without movement, the three green-clad men had inched away from each other. Masks turned their immobile dragon snouts toward their fellows. Guns moved in imperceptible arcs, ready to spit flame at the first sign of treason. One man backed square against the plaster mockery of the plague. His hand trembled on his gun.

A NEW voice broke from the trio, suddenly, hoarse with quick fear.

"There are only three of us here. There should be six."

Some one countered. "One is dead, stricken by the plague. Another turned coward, and was electrocuted." The voice hesitated, muttered an inaudible oath.

"That makes five," insisted the other. "Where is the sixth?"

A shuddering moan broke from the frightened masqueraders. It was true. There had been six green men. Now there were only five. What had happened to the sixth?

A voice cried hoarsely.

"We were six to start. Rufus Trumbull, Fisher Duane, Oliver Brearley, William Seton, Curtis Ledyard, and Paul Carrel. Let us unmask and discover who is dead, who has disappeared."

"Never!" said another hollowly. "We have bound ourselves not to unmask until midnight. No matter what might happen. The first one to do so dies."

The green mask near the bloated statue suddenly lifted his gun.

"Damn you! Damn you all!" he screamed. "I see it all now. It's my money you want. You think to kill me, kill us all. But you won't, you won't. I know you behind that mask."

The automatic jerked in his hand. The smashing concussion boomed through the hall. The middle figure spun slowly around, his mask a thing of dreadful immobility, and fell face forward.

His murderer backed against the seated death, brandishing his weapon. There was a note of triumph in his voice.

"I got him. It was he who started all this. Rip off his mask and you'll find—"

He bounded convulsively forward. His words bit off in a strangled scream. The gun fell with heavy clatter to the floor. His green-gloved hands clawed for his throat, tore feverishly at the mask. The sole surviving one in green lowered his gun, sprang nimbly away from contact with the staggering sufferer. The first rush of horrified maskers stopped in its tracks, ebbed away in frantic haste. Gail held on to Steve desperately as he lunged forward.

"Keep away!" she cried frantically. "The plague has struck him. One touch and you will die too."

Steve mouthed a bitter curse. "He was going to tell the name of the dead man when it got him. I'll rip off his mask myself."

The stricken man's screams rose to a high, keening note. His body was swelling, puffing out with the quickly generated gases of the disease. His mask jerked awry, disclosing green-ghastly features.

Gail cried sharply:

"Oh God, it's Seton!"

Then he was down, strangling and thrashing on the floor.

"Quick," Steve cried. "Who were the other two whose names were just mentioned?"

Gail steadied her trembling body.

"Paul Carrel's a doctor. Ledyard's a mining engineer who discovered the new gold lode. He claimed it was his by right of discovery. The others denied it. As for Dr. Carrel, he—My God! Listen to that!"

High above the wails and cries of the maddened maskers came a burst of laughter. It rose from nowhere, eerily muffled, yet it filled the great room with its awful clamor. A fearful, shrinking hush fell on them all at the sound. Then a huge distorted voice:

"Dupes! Idiots! Cringe before your master, Death! You mocked at him, not knowing he was in your midst. I move among you, unknown, chuckling silently. I might be your next neighbor and you'd know it not. My breath is the plague and my brushing garments corruption. By midnight not one of you shall be alive!"

The tremendous voice died down in ghastly chuckling. The maskers moaned in fear, fell away from each other with trembling haste. Who knew what outward garments hid the fleshless skull of the destroyer?

STEVE raked the room with desperate eyes, trying in vain to find the source of that curious voice. Everywhere, blank drapes met his vision. He was helpless, unknowing where the plague would strike next. But the sole survivor in green uttered a muffled exclamation. He jerked across the floor, gun lifted, shouldering the shuddering maskers from his path.

Gail cried tremulously. "The lights, Steve! They're darkening!"

It was true. The shifting kaleidoscope of ghastly colors from the chandelier had dimmed to a purple glow. Now they were fading fast, through violet, indigo—and suddenly they blanked out into the blackness of the grave.

In the viewless murk that surrounded them, someone shouted with rage. Orange flame spurted; an automatic barked. Then the same chuckle lifted itself into the blackness, obscene, sinister.

Steve gripped Gail tightly.

"Stay close to me," he whispered. "Hell is about to pop loose."

He felt the girl's body as it pressed against his. It was icy cold. A hush had fallen on the ballroom. Little pantings as men and women tried to stifle the sounds of their breathing, tiny rustlings as they edged away from contact with their fellows. Death was among them, ready to strike.

"The fools!" Steve groaned bitterly. "If only they wouldn't move, I'd hear him."

His heart was loud in his breast. He was afraid, not for himself, but for the girl who clung to him. It was she the killer would be after. Her share in the mines was considerable. If only he had a weapon; if only he had his flash. He had dropped it in his wild race through Cross Bones Gulch when the plague-stricken creatures had pursued him.

A toneless shriek of agony ripped through the rustling dark.

"Death touched me. I'm dead; I'm dead!" The screamings strangled, died away. At once another cried out. "The plague! It's like a needle. Oh, my God! My flesh is on fire; it's swelling! Help! Help!"

Mad fear swept the cavernous room. Men and women clad in fantastic costumes raced through the utter lightlessness in panic haste to get away from the death that stalked them. They crashed blindly into each other. They trampled the weak and fallen ruth'essly underfoot. They stumbled and cried out and rose again. A blinding flash, a shrill shriek of agony, the stench of sizzling flesh, told when some one touched all unknowing the death-dealing doors and windows. And through it all the plague moved on sinister feet, and masker after masker screamed horribly, and died in swollen torment.

Gail was moaning softly.

"Ssh!" Steve whispered. "Our only chance is to keep absolutely still. The killer locates his victims by their movements."

She shuddered convulsively and was silent. Steve's brain was a whirling horror. All around him men and women were dying terribly, murdered by an unseen, merciless killer, while he stood helpless, hopeless, waiting Gail's turn.

Gail screamed suddenly:

"Steve, something's touching me! Steve! Steve!"

Dread pierced his limbs as he swung savagely around. His left hand gripped her close, his right flailed out into the darkness. It met nothing. A heavy weight crashed on the back of his head. Blinding lights exploded in his brain. He heard, or thought he heard, as he fell, the faint cries of Gail as she was dragged away, the harsh chuckle of death himself. Then blackness enveloped him.

CHAPTER FOUR

The Corpse's Burning Embrace

A BLOOD-RED flame pierced Steve's pain-closed lids, forcing them open. The back of his skull ached terribly and his mouth was a dry husk. The light flared in his eyes, made him blink. It came from above, from the huge crystal chandelier. The scarlet glow beat about him in waves and made of the ballroom a bloody bath. He was on his back, arms pressed cruelly to his sides by heavy wire, legs rigid in a casing of twisted strands.

He moved his head to one side, groaning. A figure lay near by, similarly bound, unmoving. It was clad in green silk, and the sinister dragon mask stared back at him with cold ferocity. No sound came from underneath. The man was dead, or gagged.

"Now that you are both awake, we can begin," a muffled voice boomed suddenly. Steve moved his head painfully around.

A red haze swam before his eyes. Through it he saw the raised dais, and the monstrous, seated representation of the plague-stricken corpse. Thus close, he saw that its bloated limbs were made of grey paper composition and its head a huge hollow of green plaster. The eyes were empty holes into the inner void.

Even as he stared in muddled dizziness the great figure split longitudinally along its belly and swung open on well-oiled hinges. A creature stepped out on the platform; small, dapper, clad in the semblance of a devil, with scarlet hood and gilded horns. Steve blinked at him. He seemed to remember seeing that strange figure before.

It came to him suddenly. This was the masker who first had voiced the thought that death was one of them, spreading the corruption of the plague as he moved about. Then the killer hadn't been one of the six in green! They too were victims,

even as the others, of this fiend whose outward cloak portrayed all too truly the evil within.

A wild fear coursed through Steve's aching head.

"Gail!" he cried out. Where was she? Was she lying even then in the shambles, a bloated, shapeless thing of bursting grey limbs and mottled green head?

"Gail!"

A faint moan answered him. He twisted in the direction of that sound, heedless of the cruel wires that cut viciously into his flesh at every move. She was lying on the dais, at the very feet of the grisly statue and on one side of the devil mask. Her golden hair was loose and rippling over the edge of the platform, her head was back and her white throat a taut, curving line. Her parted lips made spasmodic, moaning sounds, and her eyes were closed.

"Yes, take a good look at her," the hooded demon said with a chuckle of satisfaction. "She and that stupid one in green are the last of those who owned the mines, whose wills were jointly made. Except for myself. When they are dead, I shall be sole owner, heir to millions. And no one will suspect me. I've worked it right."

Steve saw the green figure beside him shudder. He was alive then. Cold sweat beaded on his own forehead. Fire tore at his vitals. He writhed desperately in his bonds, straining with all his might. If only he could free himself, leap upon the monster before he killed the girl. The dapper devil watched his futile efforts attentively. Behind that sardonic mask he evidently was amused at the unavailing struggles of his victim.

"You'll only hurt yourself," he observed with mocking solicitude. "I do a very thorough job."

It was only too true. Steve fell back panting and groaning with pain. The wires slashed his flesh to ribbons and held with cruel tightness. It was impossible to free himself.

"Now that you've resigned yourself to the inevitable," the red-clad figure remarked approvingly, "we'll proceed. You see, I am posssssed of a naturally tender heart. I didn't wish to change this lovely girl into a hideous monstrosity like the others. In fact I would have preferred to keep her loveliness for myself."

The eyeholes in his cowl burned on the limp body of the girl, on the white bosom from which her queenly robes had been ripped half away.

"But," he went on regretfully, "she really has to die. Otherwise, by the terms of the will, she would share Cross Bones Gulch with me. So I am going to kill her painlessly. This charming statue has been wired, unknown to the others. Once she is enclosed within, the current will cook her to a crisp and tender morsel. It's a pity the process can't be observed, but—"

He shrugged red shoulders, bent down, lifted the limp, half conscious girl and thrust her into the yawning hollow of the ghastly figure. Then his foot stamped and the mechanism closed, swallowing from sight the victim within.

RED madness descended then on Steve. He shouted and screamed and cursed and jerked insanely over the floor. Blood spurted from his straining flesh, flowed redly over the steel-strong wires. But the agony of his body was as nothing to the wild torture in his brain. Gail, the girl he was to marry, whom he adored, was about to die a hideous death, and he could do nothing to save her.

The hooded devil paused with scarlet hand on a tiny button concealed in the statue's grisly belly.

"There, there," he reproved. "I'm surprised at you. I thought you'd be thankful that I didn't make of her one of those horrors that litter this room." His finger contracted to press the disk.

"Just a moment!" Steve called.

He had suddenly relaxed, was speaking with desperate calm. He had seen something. A figure was crawling slowly across the polished floor, weaving drunkenly in and out of the sprawling, mountainous corpses, dragging its scaly fish tail behind like a broken rudder. Its white mask was uplifted, and a long knife slid along, gripped by a jerking hand. Lora Trumbull, wife of Rufus!

The devil turned at Steve's call. His finger still rested on the button. His back was to the crawling, broken woman in the travesty of a mermaid costume.

"Well, what is it?" His voice was edged with impatience.

Steve's brain was a hammering madness. He must engage the demon, keep his finger from that circuit-closing button, hold his attention concentrated so he would not hear or see that inching figure. He must talk quickly.

"I admit defeat," he said evenly. By a miracle of will he kept the anguish from his voice. "You were cleverer than any of us. It was a beautiful plan. But there was only one flaw."

God! If he could only hold him like that for another minute or two!

The masked devil peered sharply down at him.

"What is that?" he demanded.

Steve's mind moved with lightning rapidity. "This," he stated in casual tones. "You didn't kill everyone who was here. Some escaped. They saw you, will bring back police. You as sole survivor under the joint instrument will naturally be under instant suspicion. They will hang you."

The figure relaxed easily. For a moment, it seemed, Steve's random shots had told. He even laughed mirthlessly.

"You've been guessing," he accused. "As

a matter of fact I *did* let some of the maskers escape. I told you I was a tender-hearted man. I slew only those whose names were signed to the will. Then I shut off the current through the doors and windows, and let the others get out. You should have seen them stampede. Of course some were unavoidably killed; others no doubt will catch the plague in the village. But a few *will* break through."

Steve shook his head in bewilderment. He almost forgot the tortured figure of the crawling mermaid, coming steadily closer. Was the killer crazy? Not for an instant did he believe the mockery of his tender heart. Why had he let any escape? Why? Why?

Suddenly he ground his teeth in savage rage. The whole horror of the fiendish plot burst upon him. Over and over again it had been emphasized through the Masque of Death that one of the green clad men had been responsible. Their names were known. The true murderer was not one of them. It would be easy afterwards, with witnesses living, to prove that point, to claim that one of the six was the actual plotter. Had not one been shot and killed by another of the six under that very accusation? The real criminal would easily escape suspicion. "You—you damnable devil!" he groaned.

"Exactly," bowed the other. "It's a compliment. I see you've understood. But now to get on with business. I have much to do yet."

He turned to the grey corpse-belly before him.

"Wait, wait!" Steve shouted frantically. "There is something else—"

But the red-shrouded demon shook his head impatiently. "You're growing tiresome. I'll have to dispose of you next, after your sweetheart."

His finger stabbed toward the button.

Behind him rose suddenly a dreadful vision. Lora Trumbull, her white mask streaked with blood and filth, her left leg dragging, broken and useless, her green mermaid's tail foul with dabbled gore. The knife glittered in her upraised hand.

"Die, Rufus Trumbull!" she screamed. "Die for the murder of my beloved Oliver."

The keen blade flashed just as the doomed man swung around. It plunged slanting into his chest, through devil's garments and ribs beneath. Bright-red blood spread in a gruesome stain. A strangled sound choked from within the hood; a red-gloved hand clutched at his breast as if to stanch the flow. Then he slid slowly to the platform.

LORA tore at her mask with her free hand, ripped it off. For a moment she tottered and swayed, glaring unseeingly at the shambles in the hall. Her puffy face still held traces of a former beauty. She flung out an arm against the statue to steady herself, missed and went plunging with a fearful scream over the edge. There was a crunching sound as her head hit the floor. Her neck vertebrae had snapped.

Steve hurled himself frantically from side to side. The silent figure next him was twitching in short spasms. A hoarse, sterterous breathing issued from the dragon head.

"Gail!" Steve shouted. "Are you still alive? Answer me."

But there came no answer from the hollow figure. God! Was it possible she—?

Then the gruesome statue swung open, and Gail darted out with a little cry. Her eyes widened on the gory scene before her, clung momentarily to the bound body of her lover. Then she was racing down from the dais, working with frantic fingers at the bonds that held him.

"There—there's a button inside that dreadful statue," she whispered as she worked. "He must have hidden in there to jab his needle of plague-germs into the poor fellow who leaned against it. All the controls for the lights are inside, too."

Steve swayed slowly to his feet, held her tight against his hammering heart.

"Gail darling!" he said over and over.

Then his eyes hardened on the masked devil figure.

"Rufus Trumbull reaped a fitting reward. His own wife killed him."

A smothered groan startled him, whirled him around. It was the prisoner in dragon head and green silk.

"Good Lord!" he muttered. "I clean forgot about him. The only one of them all, besides yourself, who has remained alive."

It took some seconds to loose his tight-clasped bonds. He wobbled upward, tearing at his dragon's head. The snarling mask fell to the ground. A wad of tight-rolled cloth spit from his mouth. Simultaneous exclamations of astonishment burst from Steve and Gail. That sardonic face, pale now with remembered death, that close-cropped mustache!

"Rufus Trumbull!"

Gail's guardian lifted a trembling hand, passed it across his brow. Then he bowed with recovered cynicism, his pose resumed.

"Yes, the murderer, the plotter, the what-have-you." His eyes went inscrutably to the broken body of his wife, who died in the thought she had slain her husband. Perhaps it was a tremor that passed over his countenance. If so, it was quickly gone.

"But who then—" Gail burst out, and stopped short. It was a question better left unasked.

Steve was already on the platform. He caught hold of the vermilion mask, ripped. A small dark face grimaced up at him, weazened and burnt with many tropic suns. An unknown face.

But Gail and Trumbull, right behind

him, knew. Their voices blended in sharp surprise.

"Doctor Carrel!"

Trumbull sucked in his breath, nodded gravely.

"I'm beginning to see," he explained. "Paul Carrel is one of the lesser stockholders. He returned only a month ago from middle Africa. He had been terribly sick out there, in some remote native village, and barely managed to pull through. No doubt it was from the plague. He's been acting pretty queerly since he's been home, now that I think of it. The disease must have done things to his mind."

Trumbull's eyes wandered slowly over the shambles that was his house.

"I'm guessing now, but I'm pretty sure I'm right," he continued. "Carrel brought a culture of the germs back with him for experimental purposes. I remember, just before the plague broke out in Cross Bone Gulch, he was called to the village to treat a sick child. In his professional bag were tubes of the deadly stuff. Whether by accident or by design, no one will ever know, the child became infected. The plague spread like wildfire."

Gail's guardian shivered, gulped.

"That was where my share of the blame comes in. I suggested this silly, ghastly Masque. I thought I was being brave and defiant and making a magnificent gesture. And it was poor Duane who thought of a joint will. Another gesture of defiance. Then it was that the frightful plot must have been born in Carrel's twisted mind. He was poor—that is, compared to the rest of us. Here was his chance to reap millions. It was he who suggested the crowning defiance of King Plague, the representation of a corpse. He fashioned it himself; he was an amateur sculptor.

"We didn't know it was hollow, or that it could open."

"Yes," Steve interrupted, "and it was

he who sent the telegram to Gail with your name to it. He wanted her share too. And then, figuring I might come to inquire, he put up that barricade to get me out of the way."

"But I don't understand," Gail protested bewilderedly. "He was originally one of the green dragon-maskers. Every one knew it. How then did he—"

"I can explain that," Steve interposed. "He was fiendishly clever in his perverted way. That was the reason he let some of the party escape. Before they got out, he must have deliberately exposed himself to their frightened eyes in his devil's costume. He had kept it hidden in another room, slipped out and donned it when the confusion started. Accordingly, the men in green would be considered guiltless. Then he'd clothe one of the unrecognizable corpses with his red mask, re-don his former green silk, and pretend he'd been knocked unconscious earlier in the evening."

Gail flung her arms suddenly around Steve's neck. "Please," she implored.

"Let's get out of this horrible place at once."

Her lover nodded grimly.

"We'd better, before we become infected. But where can we go?"

Trumbull said:

"We can camp in one of the other houses until the plague burns itself out, or help comes. Come, my dear." He offered his arm gallantly to the girl. "You and I as sole survivors are rich now; terribly so."

But she shrank slightly from him, clung closer to Steve as they moved cautiously through the fantastic dead. She could not forgive her guardian's cynicism, his lightness in the face of horrors, his seeming indifference to the tragedy of his own life.

Trumbull saw the gesture and smiled sardonically. He followed the young couple with a tiny shrug of his shoulders. He was what he was, and he was too old to change now. As for Lora—she had played him false with Oliver Brearley, had thought she had killed him. It served her right. Yet a little regretful quiver went through him at the shining devotion in those youngsters' eyes ahead, their passionate absorption in each other. His past life seemed suddenly a thing of waste and ashes. Perhaps, if there had been a Gail when he was young—

But then, he grimaced, he had never been like Steve.

THE END

GODDESS OF EVIL REVELRY

by Frederick C. Davis
(Author of "The Coming of the Mad Ones," etc.)

It was a wine more potent by far than any vintage mere mortals should ever know—a wine only pagan gods could drink with impunity. Yet it was the heady liquid of life to Hobart Forsythe—until it summoned to his side the beautiful and deadly Goddess of Evil Revelry. . . .

In Weird-Menace # 1. $5 per copy.

THE CHAIR WHERE
TERROR SAT

*A Frankly Daring Novelette of
Unholy, Deadly Lust.*

New York City, N. Y.
December 3, 1935.

I hereby certify that on this date I visited the death-house at Ossining, New York, accompanied by L. Ron Hubbard and Ed Bodin as witnesses, and did, while sitting in the electric chair, conceive this story which I have titled, "The Chair Where Terror Sat."

Arthur J. Burks

Subscribed and sworn to before me this date, December 4, 1935.

Edward F. Donovan, Notary Public, No. 104.

By ARTHUR J. BURKS

(Author of "The Women Loved by Death," etc.)

AN "ON-THE-SPOT" STORY

A CHILL wind whipped through the echoing corridors as I went into Sing Sing to die.

Outside the air had been cold, but it had been warm compared to this. Outside one could taste the whine of the wind. In here one smelled the odor of death, the agony of the ostracized.

I felt their thoughts.

They ducked, when I met them, **into**

What terror would tear your soul if you sat in the electric chair just as a joke—suddenly to feel the fatal straps tighten about you, to see the lethal electrodes clap your bared leg and shaven head, to hear the gibbering gibes of the four hundred who had died before you answer your helpless, hopeless shrieks for mercy?

their holes in the cold stone walls. My footfalls echoed along those corridors, as did those of the men who walked beside me, and those who walked behind, and before.

Our feet made a horrible, hollow sound, as though they strode across some mausoleum's roof.

My guards made a sort of ceremony of it. They stopped at an office, where there were clerks dressed in gray, handling papers, talking over telephones. But these scarcely noticed me, or my quaking knees. They must have seen many go this way.

A door. A cobbled way. Then a door with iron bars. No windows on this side of the death-house. Men should not watch, even through bars, the agony of those who will go tomorrow. It is a place of silence, of silence which now and then is rent asunder when someone's nerves snap. Then there is a shriek, broken short off, as though the one who shrieked had bitten through his lips to taste the blood of agony.

The ritual.

Nobody said anything as the turnkey set his key in the lock, and opened the door. Then he closed it. We were in a foyer, a box-like room of a place, done in faded oak. The turnkey stepped to the next door, which had no bars—because, of course, bars meant nothing to those prisoners who once entered the place. He opened the second door.

The electric chair jumped at me, like a four-legged spider, sprawled, with mouth agape, to swallow me. A chill which was never of the wind, or the cold breath of winter, or the whispering through the chill corridors, crawled slowly, horribly, down my spine . . . like icy, whitish slime.

We entered, ever so slowly, the place of death.

Two men were with me. They were my friends. And too, there was the man

whom others shunned, the executioner. His face was glum. If he had ever smiled none had ever seen him. Six other men, the six who set the straps in place. They had done all this, so many times before.

Somehow, with slow and dragging pace, and mind too numb to really know, I stepped to the chair, looked down at it. Worn were its arms. It was a rough chair, built for utility. Straps for each of the ankles, for the wrists, the elbows, one for the hips, one for the chest.

How horribly callous they were about it!

I heard myself whisper:

"How many have died here?"

"About four hundred," said the turnkey, "during the last twenty years."

Twenty a year, one every third week or less. The turnkey who explains things, took the strap that goes across the chest, and said:

"Sometimes they hit it so hard it breaks. Notice how it's stretched between the holes!"

He goes on further. The man who does the work—*the* work—goes to the door to the right of the chair, where the panel is, with the switch, and the knobs he turns for the volts and the amperes . . . 2300 volts, eight amperes. I look at the man and shiver, remembering that he hasn't smiled.

Over the door to the left rear is a sign which says: SILENCE!

The other side of that door, they tell me, is green! And beyond it the prisoners await their turn.

"Two will go tomorrow," says the turnkey. "Fish goes January 5 . . . you know, Grace Budd . . ."

I shiver again. On the way here they have taken me through the room of flouroscopy, and shown me the X-ray of Fish's body, with the stomach filled with pins and needles. Queer man, Fish. And soon he dies, in this same chair.

"These two cords, like rubber tubing," says the turnkey, "with the wire through their centers . . . see this wire?"

I looked, feeling sick inside. The points of wire were so tiny, to hurl men into eternity. I nodded.

"This wire goes into a wet sponge, fastened to the ankle of the condemned. This one goes into the hood above his head, into another wet sponge against his skull . . ."

It makes me sick, because this place of death is so grim, and silent, and *final*. Then he takes me to the panel . . .

"Here the executioner stands, waiting for the signal from the warden, after the six men have fastened the condemned in the chair. He fiddles with the knobs. At the nod he slams the switch home, and holds it for two minutes. Then, at signal, he pulls the switch, and waits while the doctor looks the man or woman over . . . if more is needed, we jam it to him!"

Horrible, the things they say to torture me, in spite of the door marked silence, beyond which the waiters wait. I can feel them listening. I can feel their agony, see their twisting hands so white with sweat and constant twisting. Then, the next room, of white tables . . . and one that slopes down to the middle, where there is a hole, and buckets scattered around, to catch things when the autopsy decreed by law is done.

I LOOKED at the buckets, the tables, and my eyes went to a black room off the autopsy room, which the eye of the condemned cannot see from the chair. In that room are coffins, rough coffins of pine, painted gray. There are trays, with head-rests . . .

"We keep 'em a few days, until the relatives claim them. If they don't, we take 'em upstate a way, and bury them. Pine box? What difference does it make, when one is dead? It wouldn't matter if you dumped them in a hole in the yard. Well, are you ready?"

I nodded. I found it hard to speak. Two other men must go tomorrow.

I went back to the chair.

They strapped me in. The executioner stood at the panel, just as he always does when a man gets set to die. The six stand back. My friends, with faces white and sweating, stepped back, too. Dimly, in the row of seats to the left, before me, I could see the faces of the twelve witnesses, who were not really there.

They strapped me in. They left, all save the executioner, who fiddled with his panel. This is all so real, understand? I have just come through the little green door, and am being strapped in. My skull is shaved for the electrode, and my ankle. I am tightly bound in place. The others left, save the executioner.

Passing me, on the way out, he paused long enough to change the lights, so that just one, and that one dim, looked down upon me from above. His face, as he looked into mine, his back to the others, who wait for him, but are impatient to begone—his grim face twisted into ax grimace.

"So, you would tell the world of this, eh? And they will wonder about the man who does it! Well, you'll never tell them, understand, because this thing you are doing will be more real than you could ever have dreamed!"

Looking into his face I wanted to scream. But my tongue clove to the roof of my mouth, and words would not come over my dry lips. He didn't hurry, even then. He asked a question:

"Remember Becker?"

"Becker?" I had to repeat it by shaping my lips, for his face made me mute with abysmal terror.

"Yes, Becker. Gyp the Blood, Leftie Louie—"

Then I nodded.

"Well, one day he sat in that chair

and joked about it. A year later we strapped him into it, and he didn't joke—not when I pushed home the switch."

God, I could have risen then. I tugged against the straps, to get away, to be free of this place of horror. But the straps, those eight straps of doom—to hold a man tight in the face of death—held me now, as, over twenty years, they or others like them, had held a full four hundred. Their names flashed through my mind. I started to mumble them, but terror made me stop, asking myself a question:

"*Suppose you called them, and they came?* For you sit at the gateway, where men can look two ways—and *see!*"

Then the gross man, thick and sturdy, with pasty face, strode out and left me, there alone in the chair where so many had died. His words stuck in my mind, and stunned it:

"*It will be more real than you ever dreamed!*"

What in God's name had he meant? I twisted my head to look. Through the gloom I could see the panel, and the switch. At my feet was the point of wire for the ankle, fully two feet from my flesh. Behind me somewhere, dangling down the chair, was the wire for the skull.

They didn't touch me. The switch could not be pushed. *Hands* must do that, must affix the electrodes, and there were no hands here now but mine—and those, of course, of the man in the ice-box, in the room to my right, which I had seen but could not see—the man who had sat here two nights ago.

Behind me, to the left, the door marked SILENCE. Beyond that door . . . I listened.

Creepy sounds came through that door, and through the wall of dark the shade over my dim light had made . . . creepy sounds, as though those who waited just beyond, had come to the door of green to listen. They knew I was here, they must know. They had no interest in knowing how it felt to die. They would know tomorrow—*any* tomorrow!

To my right, grim reminders of those who had gone before, four hundred of them. To my left, through that door, those who would go tomorrow. The four hundred had sat as I sat. Eighteen were destined now, beyond all peradventure, to go tomorrow, or the day after or—what did it matter when?

I sat, sweat trickled down my face. The whispers were everywhere, like soft wings. The black door to the autopsy room was a whale's mouth, opened for flesh. White tables there were like ghosts, asleep.

Not a sound . . .

But yes, there were sounds. From behind me, to the left. The door marked SILENCE was opening, slowly, softly. Whispering came to my ears. They'd told me that door was locked! Great God, did those who were doomed to die, come here to hold high revelry when all the lights were out? I must be dreaming.

Yes, it must be a nightmare, for now in the autopsy room I heard a sound that chilled me to the marrow. Ice rubbing against ice, as though the dead had turned and sighed with cold, and turned again.

I heard a gentle footfall, in among the tables . . .

And then I saw him, standing there in the door.

His head was shaved. His leg was slit. His skull was burned and his leg was burned.

His face was grey.

His clothes were grey.

His skull was shaved.

His trouser leg was slit.

CHAPTER TWO

Hell's Laughter

SAVE for the burns, and the cropped hair, and the slitted trousers, he looked much like other men. But those eyes of his! They bored into and through me. He hated me, I could see, with a deep and deadly hatred. I wondered why. I wondered even more when, from the darkness behind him, came the soft sound of a woman's sobbing. Strange, terrible, eerie sobbing, out of the dark. The man whose face I had once seen in the newspapers of the land, turned and spoke over his shoulders:

"Don't cry, dearest. I'll take care of the matter!"

Behind me, where I couldn't see, because I could not twist far enough, came a burst of cackling laughter. High, shrill, nervous. I could fancy the man who laughed, biting his fingers until they bled, his eyes so wide with terror they, too, almost bled. I could see a human being standing there, twisting, writhing like a snake, watching me, sitting here, as he would one day sit.

The man in the door of the autopsy room spoke to the man who laughed behind me:

"You shouldn't trouble," he said, and named a name I knew so well, because it was fresh in the news. "It's all quickly over. It isn't bad, really."

"No, maybe not—" the answer was a shrieking shout, broken, battered, as though the voice were a gull that smashed against a cliff and, wheeling, reeling, caught itself again and flew again, mewing, into some abysmal storm—"but this horrible, horrible, waiting! Why do they torture me so?"

"Because you killed . . ."

And the man in the door named the person the shouter had killed.

"But I didn't! I didn't!"

"I know you didn't, but the law said you did, and all the shouting you can do won't make them say anything else. Not now. I know who did the killing."

"You do? Then tell! Tell!"

"Sorry, I can't cross this threshold. You know that, don't you? A fellow just travels one way across this sill."

"Oh, God, I recognize you now. I read about you, and condemned you, and said you deserved what you were getting, you and the woman with you. I never dreamed it could happen to me. But it did —will—and I didn't kill anybody! And how is it that I see you?"

"Because we are very close, you and I. And both of us are close to this sweating, terrified man who sits in the chair where I sat, where you will sit tomorrow —Look at him! How do you think he would feel if he knew, positively, as you know, that he's really going to get it? I wonder. But it won't happen. He'll go out, and tell about it. He'll use the scalpel of words upon our souls. He'll strip us naked, again and again, for the world to see."

"And I, too—and none of my people know that I am coming through this door again tomorrow. Can't we stop this— this—ghoul?"

I managed to interrupt. I had to, or scream.

"That door," I said, my voice strange, frightening, there in the gloom, "how could anyone get through it? I thought it was locked."

"It is, my friend, but what are locks and bars to the soon-to-die? Understand me, now. They are really beyond that door, the whole eighteen of them, but every day, every hour, every minute, in their agonized minds, they quit their cells, come to the green door, open it, step through, are grabbed by the six men, three to a side, and strapped in that chair you occupy, their bodies taut, their minds numb, as they meet their Maker face to face."

"You mean, he isn't real?"

"As real as you. As real as I. But only you can see, or hear, either of us. That's because you sit in a door that looks both ways."

"And the others? The four hundred?"

"Oh, they're around. They haven't had time to go far, any of them. They're rather aimless, undecided about things. It all happened so suddenly, you know. They can never make up their minds about anything. But you know why they went, don't you?"

"Yes, they killed someone—and were killed in turn."

"Right. And they can, and will, kill again—only now they cannot *die!* Now they can punish those who punished them, and never be punished again!"

"Great Scott, what do you mean?"

"Society. The people. Not many ever come, and sit there, as you sit, and give us such a break as this. But one did. Before my time it was. His name was Becker."

"But you can't cross that threshold. You said so yourself."

"I do not need to, my friend," said the standing corpse in grey. "Many things are possible without crossing thresholds. Look, down at the naked wire, two feet from your ankle."

How I dreaded to look down! But his voice was so insistent. I looked. His eyes, filled with ghastly things, had made it impossible for me not to look. That wire—with the snaky length of tubing—my eyes found it, caught, held!

And, like the snake to which I had likened it, the wire moved toward my right ankle, undulating, and stopped, six inches closer to my leg than it had been!

A dreadful, ghastly screaming rang through the chamber of death. It came from everywhere, began everywhere. My lips were wet, and when I realized that, I knew it had been I who had screamed.

I BIT my lips to keep from coming again. But the scream continued. It still came from everywhere, but I ran it to earth, and knew, at last, whence it really came—through that door marked SILENCE!

The eighteen condemned to die were screaming—and little wonder! For out of the ghastly place, beyond the door which, to them, was green, had come my scream—from the place where they had heard nothing, ever, save silence, and a dynamo humming through, now loud, now soft. The condemned did not scream, because their lips were dry, and their tongues were dry, and their brains were made of ashes.

Yet I had broken the night asunder with my scream.

Now came other screams!

"Why don't you get it over with?"

"Great God! What goes on in there?"

"Mother of Jesus! Hasn't someone a pill, or a knife . . . I can't stand this waiting?"

And the others, who did not scream or cry out, answered those who did with laughter—ghastly, chattering laughter, like that of apes gone mad in a pit of hell.

The man in the door to the black room of the white ghosts sleeping, smiled a little, a spine-crawling smile, and nodded toward the door behind me.

"No one, even I, could ever make them believe it didn't matter," he said.

"Nor could I," I managed to mutter. "I'd go mad!"

"What good would it do?" The bars hold you. The straps never break—except sometimes when the bodies are jammed against them by the power of the juice, but by that time they're too dead to think or care."

Why did he have to remind me of the

straps? I would be here until morning. I looked down at those straps. Those on my ankles—looking at them, I couldn't avoid looking at the naked wire in the tubing . . .

It was inches closer to my ankle than it had been when I had last looked!

I went crazy. I lurched against the straps, with all my power.

"I wouldn't," I heard the strange visitor say, "the law can drive you against them harder! And it will hurt less!"

I leaned to the left, over that arm of the chair which is worn more deeply than the other. I leaned to the right. I leaned back, banging my head. I lurched forward. I moved with all my power, And nothing happened. The straps snapped, and their snapping was a kind of hideous laughter that drove me even deeper into the pit of horror.

When I finally stopped for lack of breath, my lips were bleeding, and crimson rolled down over my chin. My wrists were bleeding, too, and so were both my ankles. I was raw and sore from the wounds of my madness.

"You see?" said my visitor. "It's no use. You can't budge them."

"Come over! Unfasten them, for the love of God!"

"I told you I couldn't come back," he said, strangely.

"But you—whatever moved the electrode—can move the straps . . ."

He grinned. His grin was ghoulish, horrible, and his face was so other-worldly grey.

"But of course," he said. "Watch! The left ankle—"

I looked down. There were no hands that I could see. But the flap of the strap moved, backed as though of its own accord, out through the buckle. I felt the strap tighten as it pulled to let the metal tongue escape the hole in the leather. Good, it could be done I might not escape this place of horror, but out of that ghastly chair—

And then I screamed again. Even to me its sound was horrible.

For with a swift, savage wrench, as though done by the hand of a gorilla, the belt *tightened another hole!* It cut into my flesh like a razor. It was a wonder it did not break the bone itself. I stared in amazement, in utter, abysmal terror. Escape was possible, or had been—but now, never. For some grim, ghastly reason, I was more tightly a prisoner than ever.

And out of the black room came the sound of laughter—and then a woman speaking, through her sobs:

"Haven't you done enough?"

"He deserves it, said the man, out of the dark. "I only slew. He paws over the dead like a ghoul, and slays, and slays again."

Then he came back to stand in the door, leaning against the jamb on one leg, the foot whose ankle was burned rubbing the knee of the other.

"We'll be ready for you, in a minute, snooper!" he said. "I've just sent for my neighbors! Remember what the executioner—jolly fellow, isn't he—said when he left? That this would be more real than you could even guess? He knew, of course, and why not? Who among the living, could be closer to us than he is?"

"What in heaven's name are you going to do?"

"You wanted to find out, as nearly as possible, what it meant to be electrocuted, didn't you? Well, we're going to show you! *Before witnesses, four hundred of them!*"

CHAPTER THREE

The Agony of Preparation

HE laughed a little, lightly—too lightly. I stared at him through the mist of sweat which dripped from my forehead.

"You didn't play fairly," he said. "You didn't go through the worst of it."

"What worst?"

"The time of waiting for actions on appeals. The moving up, from room to room, each one closer to the green door. The last day, when you wait just beyond it. You must, to know the truth, go through that, you know. BEGIN!"

He lifted his right hand, as though at a signal. The fist was closed, and he seemed to hurl a blow in my direction. I felt as though I had been struck on the head with a sledgehammer, though nothing really touched me. I saw stars. A scream bubbled from my throat, for I thought someone had slammed the switch.

Then, just darkness . . .

Darkness out of which came queer, mice-like sounds. Darkness filled with the odor of agony. I opened my eyes and looked around me.

"Thank God," I thought, "I got out of that chair somehow."

Then I saw the door—and the door was green!

I was in a cell, outside the room where the chair was, in the room where the condemned experienced the agony of the day-before. Only, it seemed that all eighteen were here, nineteen counting me. I rose, like a man swimming in a fog of horror, stepped to the door of my cell, put my hands out to grasp the bars— how strangely natural the action seemed —and tried to see as many of my comrades of the death-house as I could.

Straight across from me was a young fellow, twenty or so, I judged him. I stared at him intently. He lifted a hand, negligently.

"Hi, Bud!" he said.

I tried to answer him, and couldn't. It took a little time for my fogged brain to grasp his identity. Then I knew. He had shot down a man with a tommy gun,

and behind the running man two children had been playing, and they too had gone down, riddled with bullets. He deserved to die, no doubt about that. Twenty years old, and taking the walk tomorrow, or the next day.

"Keep your chin up, Bud," he said. "The rest of us will be right behind you."

"Right behind me?" I gasped. "But I haven't done anything! I'm not going to the chair! What do you mean, right behind me?"

The fellow laughed.

"Hear that, fellows?" he said. "He claims he didn't do it. Sounds natural, don't it? And he's scared half to death. I guess he's a little screwy, that he doesn't know he's starting his walk in a couple of hours. Don't you remember, Burks? Look down at your leg and that'll remind you. I guess you must be punch-drunk, or full of hop or something."

I looked down at myself. Dressed in grey. The right trouser leg slit to the knee. I slapped my hand to my skull, to find the spot where it had been shaved.

"Yes, yes; of course," I said, "I'd forgotten that the barber had been here. And the padre, did he come?"

"Yeah. You were tough about that; told him you didn't believe in God, and didn't want him around. You lied, you know, fellah."

"He didn't lie!" screamed someone off to my right, where I couldn't see. "Of course he denied God. Do you think if there were a God he could look in here and let us go through all this? Shut up, you buzzards! Don't you know I'm going tomorrow?"

Chill along the marrow of every bone in my body. I pinched myself, and it was real. I, Arthur J. Burks, was in a cell in the death-house, in the room-before-the-last, and would be taking the walk in two hours—an hour and 55 minutes now.

I screamed.

That started them. Their nerves were raw. All were edgy. Off to my left, across the way, I heard a man chuckling. He said, finally, in a thick voice.

"Keep it up, you hounds! I like to hear you suffer. You don't know exquisite pleasure when you experience it. That's why I'm of greater clay than you are. I'm only sorry of one thing: when I go, on January 5th, I won't be able to stand aside, look down and enjoy my own suffering. But the anticipation may make up for it. I wish I'd get a reprieve, just as they fasten the straps, and then have it all to do over again, every night in the week. That, my friends, would be ecstasy!"

"Stop him! Stop him!" I thought it was the others shrieking, but it was myself. "Stop the raven's croaking!"

Up spoke a kindly, ministerial-looking man, who had made a flaming torch of his wife and buried the charred remains in a lime pit.

"We'd all best get a hold on ourselves. It isn't so bad, really, Burks. But it always nerves most of us up, when one of us gets set to go. Now be quiet, everyone. Try to make it easier for him to go!"

I bit my lips. A grumbling silence finally settled over the ghastly red-brick pile of the death-house, this tomb-before-the-tomb. I wondered why, outside, on my way in, I hadn't recognized the place by the low cloud which hovered over it, with flapping black wings, the Death Angel.

But the silence didn't last long. Up the way a bit another young chap—he'd murdered his sweetheart and a rival—began to moan, and mumble.

"Our Father Which Art in Heaven . . . Oh, God! Oh, God! Oh, God! Why doesn't someone give me something? Why don't they take me in, right now, and jolt me out of this with all the volts and amps they've got?"

Another spoke up:

"Why call on God? He can't hear you? He's got His back turned to the death-house!"

And then, for five minutes—how well I knew it was exactly five minutes—he uttered such words of blasphemy as I had never heard dribble from the lips of a man. I got a look at him finally, when he came to the door of his cell, grasped the cold bars and tried to yank them from their sockets—pulled and pulled until his clothing was blacked all over, with his sweat.

Such ghastly words!

For twenty years he had saved the souls of men and women. Then a woman's faithlessness had sent him here, because he had killed her for it, with a sharp knife drawn swiftly across her throat. He'd called the police himself, and sat beside her until they came. I remembered the pictures in the tabloids, the woman lying there, the pool upon the floor, staining the carpet.

Minutes, ticking away.

I HEARD a dynamo hum beyond the green door. The executioner was testing things, to make sure there would be no mistakes. God, it couldn't be that he was doing that for *me!* And yet—he was. Eighteen condemned men said so! In one hour and thirty minutes—just a heartbeat ago it had been two hours—I would . . .

"Mother of Jesus, I can't stand it!" I cried out.

"They all say they can't," spoke up another, "but somehow they always do."

It made me think back to words I had exchanged with the turnkey, before this had become so real, so nightmarishly real.

"Do they carry on something terrible,

when they come in? Do they fight? Do they have to be carried?"

"Naw! That's tabloid stuff. I've been here nine years. I've never seen one break. They just come in, sit down, and take it. It's the living that do the suffering! You ought to see the green faces of the newspapermen and other witnesses!"

And the turnkey's face as he remembered—and how much he could remember, of past nine years—had been a little green as he told me.

One hour left to go. A crawling, horrible hour. A fast, lightning-fast agonizing hour.

"Why, in God's name," I shrieked, "don't they just let us go to sleep, the first night we spend in this place—and simply make sure we don't wake up again?"

"Why, haven't you heard?" said the familiar, grating voice. "This is for punishment. *Your* way would be too easy. We have to meditate on our sins before we go. That's why I'm waiting until January 5th, because what I did, they said, was so unnatural, so horrible. To me it wasn't, not at all."

I looked at him. His eyes were avid. He licked his red—his too-red—lips, with ghastly enjoyment, watching my suffering, as I crucified myself against the bars.

Twenty minutes to go . . .

Fifteen minutes . . .

I shrieked for five minutes. My heart swelled and almost burst. I wished it would, and end everything. Every nerve twanged, hummed with terror.

Twelve minutes . . . God, how fast they were going!

Then, five minutes, and the first footfalls came.

I knew then, and a sort of cloud came over my mind. It was like a swift shot of dope, somehow. Those footfalls, so measured, like a squad parading—or like a funeral escort.

Then, they were standing before my cell. A chaplain was there . . . and the warden . . . and others.

But, God's blood, they were dressed in grey. Some of their faces I had almost forgotten. I had to think back, hard, to remember. But not the others there, not the eighteen. Most of them, it seemed, had studied everything about the chair they could. They'd even memorized casehistories of those who had gone before them.

That's why it didn't seem strange that one of those who stood outside my cell was a woman.

The prisoners began to name them. They started wagering. The first one to name them all would get a prize of some kind.

We were all so close together, and all so close to death, that none of it seemed strange.

But as they named my visitors, one by one, I looked down at each . . . and saw the slitted trousers. I lifted my eyes to each skull, and saw the shaved places.

Then, my door clanged, and I was stepping out, remembering . . .

"They all take the walk through the door, sit down, and take it!"

"But why should I?" I asked. "I haven't done anything."

"Neither have a million people outside, who don't even dream of the chair." It was the shaven-pated padre who spoke, sonorous, unctuous, to explain. He'd gone, years ahead of me, for throttling a baby. "But it may happen to any of them, at any time, unless they watch their step—or even if they do! Come on, the warden has a date for late dinner. He's going to get drunk to forget."

Then I was out, walking. Nobody, strangely, was holding me up. My feet took all the initiative out of my hands. That's mixed, but maybe you understand me. My feet turned, in the midst of my visitors, and pointed their curled toes at the little green door—which wasn't little at all.

We started walking. I, too, kept the funeral pace of the dead. Why not? I'd soon be of them.

"We'll be seeing all of you again!" said one of my keepers.

"Righto!" shouted the January-man. "I can scarcely wait!"

The speaker's words were none too well received. Eighteen men grabbed at the bars of their cells, and tried to shake them. Even the hard-boiled baby-killer broke a little, and tried to bite through the chilled steel. I took the sound of his rasping teeth with me, right to the green door.

The clamor was ghastly, horrible.

I started to shake hands with the condemned as I passed them.

ONLY two could shove their shaking hands through the bars. Too well they knew that shortly each of them, even as I, would be making this ghastly walk.

The green door opened. For the second time the chair jumped at me—the second time and the last!

I glanced to the left. Somehow I managed to smile.

The seats, there, were filled with people, twelve of them. Two were women, with red rimmed eyes and parted lips, and one, already, was swaying.

The faces of the others were green.

Those in the second row of seats gripped the back of the seats ahead, hard —and their knuckles were white

Those in the first row sat back, hard against the seats, and gripped their knees, because there was nothing else but empty air. They had their feet solidly planted, but wide apart, as though to brace themselves.

The warden was standing, watch in hand. He looked impatient, and a little sick. I glanced at the panels, where the robust, sturdy one stood. He grinned at me:

"I told you," he said, "that it wasn't a joking matter!"

Of all of them here, he was the only one who would be alive when this was over—and yet, madly, chaotically, he was the closest to death of all of us, for his was the master's hand which brought it, crashing like a thunderbolt.

I sat down.

Six men grabbed me, three on a side.

The straps were pulled tightly, but they didn't cover my mouth. The wet sponges dripped cold water on my leg, and on my skull. At the panel the executioner stood, grinning, eager.

The warden stared at the executioner.

I could see the white ghosts sleeping, in the black room beyond. One of them was a table I would soon be lying on, only I would not know it. There they would do dreadful things to me. The where I could see them.

The man with the grey clothing and the grey face came back to the door, looked at me and said:

"How do you like it, as far as you've gone?"

Behind him in the dark a woman wept. It must have been the same one who had come through the door with me, for I couldn't see her anywhere.

Strange what the words did to all the actors in this ghastly room.

It froze them into statues where they stood . . .

Then they began fading out, as the grey man said . . .

"Let us take it on, from here. After all, who could know all the details better than we do?"

CHAPTER FOUR

The Ampere Dance

SO began the grim, strange dance of the amps and the ods. The amperes of doom, and the ods of those who had died before me. I sat in the chair where Becker had laughed and watched it.

I knew that the executioner stood in his cubicle, ready to pull the switch that would send the lethal current hurtling through my body.

I could feel him there, gloating, and the spirits of those who had gone before me were hovering over me, and they were waiting, too.

Something hit me all over. The blow which was so hard I didn't even feel it, though it drove me through the straps as if I had been hurled from a catapult. They broke as though they had been twine, and I turned, finding myself standing upright, to see what they would do now. Strap me back in again, of course, and do it all over again.

But there was something queer here. There was someone in the chair. A man. A man with my face, and now the amps were burning him, and over him hovered the shades of his predecessors.

I was spirit now, it seemed, free from pain while there in the grisly chair was all that remained of what I had been. All about the body which burned, all about me, amidst the shades, were the phantoms of those who had gone before; gruesome, infamous names. And there too were all the "twelves" who had watched the passing of the four hundred.

I stared at the curling smoke. I smelled the odor of flesh.

The smoke was hypnotic. I felt myself sinking into something, the Pit of the damned, perhaps . . .

I CAME back to life, among the living, to find that it was dawn. I was stiff and sore. My friends said, as I was un- fastened, that my hair was greying. I didn't speak, I merely gestured feebly, as though I would have said:

"Outside, for the love of God, where a man can look on life again!"

We went out, fast. I didn't wish to hear any more whispers from the cells of the eighteen, beyond the SILENCE door. I just wanted to get out.

A whisper followed me, coming, I knew, from the cold one on the ice, in the third room of ghastliness.

"Think well, oldtimer," the whisper said, "for you may be back, you know, like Becker." I even thought I heard the sounds of Becker's laughter.

CHAPTER FIVE

The Tent of Blue

HOW glorious the prison was! Outside the death-house, I mean. I didn't look back as I stepped onto the cobblestones with my two friends. We went again into that part of the prison which is a hundred and ten years old, where the cells are kennels not fit for dogs. Or so, yesterday, I had thought.

"Here," the turnkey had said, looking down at the troughs in the stones which the feet of countless thousands had worn, down the decades of a century and more, "is where we put the newcomers. It breaks their hearts . . ."

Now I stopped and looked at some of the newcomers, with horror in their eyes, and sweat upon their faces.

"This," I told them, "is swell! It's sweller than swell! It's heaven on earth!"

"Yeah," croaked one, "says you!"

"And says you, too," I retorted, "if you'd been where I've been. It's just outside your door, too."

"Jeez," said another, "maybe the guy with the white hair knows his stuff, at that. It is sort of homey in here!"

It smelled of bodies, of stools and things, but is was homey.

Then into the new places, where there were three tiers of cells instead of six . . . and I thought: "In my Father's House are many mansions, but none could be as fine as this. Just to dawdle here, all my life, would be swell. To work my fingers to the bone, in the shops, would be a delight that would make me sing the days away."

Then back and back, heading out, my comrades silent beside me, studying me, as though I had truly been a man come back from the dead.

The cells for the short-timers—five years and under——with windows giving on the out-of-doors, with earphones over their pillows, so they could listen to the radio at night.

One cell, strangely, was open. I went into the cell. How glorious it was! I stepped to the barred window, looked out. The bars were friends, shielding me from harm. Beyond was the sunlight. And higher up—

". . . that little tent of blue, we prisoners
    call the sky,
And ever snowy cloud that drifts,
Its ravelled fleeces by. . . ."

I stood until my comrades scuffed their feet with impatience.

The turnkey said:

"Like to ride back in the Black Maria? It's faster."

Marvelous! Glorious!

The hated Black Maria! It was a chariot, with wings. Its driver, dressed in grey, was an angel—with cauliflowered ears, and hammered cheeks, but an angel just the same.

The next to the last door out. Then the last.

I stood on the flight of steps. To my left was the great black door through which so many went, never to come forth again. And through it, back to life, had many others come—to be looked at askance by folks who'd never know what fate might hide behind high walls of stone.

I stood on the steps, as I say.

My friends—I scarcely knew they were there.

The wind was in my face. I opened my mouth. It blew down my throat. I drank it in, deeply. I filled my chest with it.

I looked up at that "tent of blue," where stars wheeled in their courses, only at night. I wanted to scream to them, to shout for all the world to hear:

"How God damn beautiful you are!"

I shrugged, started along to where our car would be parked, where so many cars were parked on visiting days, so many cars had parked to await the tragic coming-forth.

My feet hammered against the pavement.

I stopped, rubbed my right sole against the pavement, and then my left. I kept at it, crazily, until absolutely sure that it was a pavement, this side the grave, and that the soles were mine, covering feet which were mine, attached to legs that were mine, attached to a living body that some men knew by name.

I kept repeating that name, over and over again, over and over.

Into the car. I fingered the upholstery. I kicked at the back of the seat. I fiddled with the starter, the gear-shift. I did something I had always hated to do, now, when there was really no reason for it.

I asked for the heavy crank. I got out and cranked the car. I told the driver to leave the ignition off, until I had cranked myself into a sweat.

Then, finally, in the car, I lowered all the windows they would let me. It was bitter cold, but the cold was lovely, gorgeous, sublime.

I stuck my hands out of the first one window, then the other. I felt of the wind. I ran it through my fingers like the beads of a rosary, over and over again. And then, something I hadn't done for ages, I prayed, from the depths of my heart, to become a better man promised to do my part to accomplish the desired end.

A restaurant . . .

And just before the food, a telegram to my people. How happy I was that the telegram could be happy! No happier one, I was sure, had ever been penned from here, sent from here. The telegram sang.

Then, food . . .

The waitress asked me:

"What do you want?"

She must have thought me crazy when I answered:

"Everything on the menu. Everything from the stores hereabouts. Bring in people for me to watch while I eat."

And then, she brought everything, and I had to pay my check without eating, because memory came rushing back, and I couldn't have eaten to save my life.

Just before we turned a corner, getting away, I looked back in the direction of the place of horror.

A black cloud, which I could see—my comrades, when I asked them, said they could see only sunlight, and the "tent of blue"—so plainly, settled slowly out of the sky down toward the roof of a building I hoped never to see again.

And I remembered something else:

Two men below that cloud, under that red-brick, dreadful roof, must go tomorrow!

I turned to the chauffeur.

"Drive!" I said. "Drive! Drive! Break all speed laws. They don't burn you for that! Drive! For my soul's sake drive."